Praise for
KEYS TO THE LAST RESORT

"Licia Rester may have found a new genre! Keys to the Last Resort *is a compelling page-turner that is also personally empowering and transformational. It's relatable and magical! It's uplifting, inspiring, and filled with surprises. It's not just a book, it's an experience!"*

~ Cindy Lou Golin, PhD, transformation coach and author of *The Shadow Playbook*

"At last! A fun, enchanting, and transformational story! This novel offers a fresh and inspiring perspective on love and relationship that will leave you feeling uplifted and inspired. Whether you're in a happy marriage or struggling to connect with your partner, this novel is a must-read for anyone seeking to unlock the magic of love and personal growth."

~ Dayna Dunbar, award-winning author of visionary fiction including *Awake: The Legacy of Akara*

"As a couple in a long-term successful marriage and both coaches ourselves, we were blown away by the wisdom and inspiration in Keys to the Last Resort. *This novel offers a unique and powerful approach to personal growth and transformation, reminding us of the power of love, forgiveness, and resilience."*

~ Dr. Kamin Samuel and Mark Samuel, international coaches, and authors

"To read Keys to The Last Resort *is to experience a journey into the very heart of the alchemy of love, and of the capacity of love's power to reinvent a romantic partnership. This very compelling story draws the reader in while also offering a remarkable context for personal transformation for both the individual and the couple. I highly recommend this novel as both an entertaining read and as an exceptionally crafted tool for self-examination and growth for couples, regardless of gender."*

~ Mark Cote, composer

"Keys to the Last Resort *reads like a fusion of the hyper-realistic and the mysteriously romantic. At no point does Licia Rester relinquish plausibility for the sake of mere romance or drama, and at no point does this story lurch from reality into realms shadowy, indeterminate, or unknowable. From beginning to end,* Keys to the Last Resort *remains grounded — grounded in reality. It is psychologically rich, emotionally complex, relatable to the core. Yet in this novel there is no suggestion of life as a tragic mode of despair and no treatment of human relationships as doomed, pointless, or cosmically absurd.* Keys to the Last Resort *is a novel of subtlety and poignancy, a novel whose theme is wildly romantic — in the true and original sense of the word: infused with reality through and through, yet stylized and filled with a sense of wonder, expectation, happiness.*"

~ Ray Harvey, bestselling author of *Whiskey Wisdom*

"*I couldn't put it down. I loved the jewels of wisdom sprinkled along the way and was fascinated by the use of mythology and how it directly linked to the protagonist's life. As a psychologist, I was particularly interested in the ways Licia Rester adapted sound psychological principles to the fantastical elements of the story. I look forward to more in this series!*"

~ Nadine Vaughan, PhD

"Keys to the Last Resort *is the perfect novelette to read poolside on a hot summer day. There is a great deal of practical relationship advice woven throughout its pages. This book is totally worth your time, whether you're reading it for fun or to deepen connections with your partner. With compelling characters and practical advice for couples, the story is both entertaining and fun.*"

~ Jana Faulkner

"As a pastor, I have seen firsthand the power of love and faith to transform lives. Keys to the Last Resort *is a powerful and inspiring novel that offers a unique blend of storytelling and principles for success, providing readers with a valuable tool for personal growth and transformation."*

~ Rev. Dr. Lisa Clayton, pastor

"From the opening paragraph, Licia Rester's novel immediately engaged me like a magnetic riptide. As the drama deftly unfolded, my inspiration to evolve grew as the characters' alienated relationship with themselves and each other shifted into meaningful love and personal fulfillment. She brilliantly illustrates how our inner resources fuel the courage and skills needed to overcome unexpected challenges."

~ Susan Forster, leadership consultant and founder of PositivityWork

"I normally think of a 'self-help' book as a chore that I need to read to solve some otherwise insoluble problem. Not so with Keys to the Last Resort. *Far from reading like a self-help book, Licia Rester's story is a delightful sprint into the problems that I'm sure many couples have, but full of fun, magic, and unexpected twists and turns. I couldn't put it down. And as someone who is often moved by tales of redemption and reconciliation, I found myself crying joyously as the protagonist Sylvia dives headfirst into the story's climax. Well done!"*

~ Arnie Richards

"Licia Rester takes you on a journey that feels like an engaging, provocative love story at the beginning but somehow expands into a bigger experience of the divine nature of love itself. Be ready to lose yourself in sweet surrender."

~ Steve Chandler, author of *Time Warrior*

"*Keys to the Last Resort integrates storytelling and proven principles for success to create a refreshing and innovative approach to personal growth and transformation. This novel offers a unique and engaging way to explore the complexities of marriage, love, and personal transformation, providing readers with a valuable resource to unlock the magic in their own lives.*"

~ Stu Semigran, president & co-founder of EduCare Foundation and author of *Heartset Education: A Way of Living and Learning*

"*Keys to the Last Resort is more than just an engaging and entertaining work of fiction. It incorporates principles of personal growth, demonstrating to readers that their choices can transform their lives and 'rewrite their story.'*"

—Erin J. Kishpaugh, freelance writer and book editor

KEYS TO THE LAST RESORT

Unlock the Magic ♦ Reawaken to Love
Are you Ready?

LICIA RESTER

Published by Paper Raven Books LLC

Printed in the United States of America

First Printing, 2023

Paperback ISBN: 979-8-9857606-4-4
Hardback ISBN: 979-8-9857606-5-1

For those who yearn to reawaken the magic of love,
Your dreams are waiting for you,
Inviting you to step through the door,
Locked so long ago.

Here is the key…

*"Some day you will be old enough to start
reading fairy tales again."*

~ C.S. Lewis

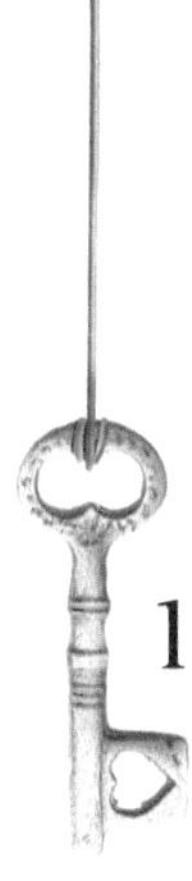

A LONG, DRY ROAD

If this were one of Sylvia's favorite childhood books, something fantastic would pull her out of her frustration and discouragement. A surprise, a new friend, even an old enemy, might interrupt the silent tension between Carl and herself as they drove to what should have been a celebratory 25th anniversary. If this were a rom-com, the fight that morning as they packed for the weekend would have been funny, peppered with witty banter, and quickly forgotten.

But her life, especially her marriage, wasn't a fantasy. All the "rom" and "com" had drained from it years ago.

"Are we close?" Sylvia wished she wasn't always the one who had to make the first move when they fought.

No response.

Sylvia pulled her gaze from the car window to her husband. Was he giving her the cold shoulder? Or had he simply not heard her—again?

"Carl." She forced herself to soften the sharpness of her tone. "Did you hear me?"

"Huh?" He kept his eyes on the road.

Sylvia's jaw clenched. Like most husbands, Carl had developed selective deafness—but only to her. She glanced at his left hand gripped on the steering wheel. His wedding ring. Not merely a symbol of love and fidelity. No, according to her pet theory, it was a short-circuiting device, blocking reception whenever she spoke, a symptom growing worse as the years progressed.

"I asked, are we close?"

He chuckled. "You sound like Gracie on one of our road trips. 'Are we there yet? How much longer?'" he said, pitching his voice to match their daughter when she was a little girl.

Her tone regained its edge as Sylvia bristled. "Forgive me for wanting to know how much longer I have to sit here in total silence."

"What silence? We're talking right now."

She threw up her hands in mock surrender. "Fine. Let's just keep arguing. It's a great way to start our anniversary weekend." Sarcasm wasn't the solution, but she couldn't help herself. The man was infuriating.

Carl sighed loudly, lifting his eyes skyward before returning to stare at the empty highway in front of them.

"What's that supposed to mean?"

But he didn't answer. Just kept staring forward.

Sylvia's hackles rose. She knew what he was playing at, but if she called him on it, he would claim he was keeping his eyes on the road for safety's sake. Of course, safety flew right out the window when he needed to look to the heavens like some kind of martyr.

Stomach churning, she bit out, "What are you trying to say, Carl? If you could just give me a clue."

"All I'm doing is driving, Sylvia. To a weekend that I spent *my* time setting up. But you're still biting my head off. That's a mystery to me. Maybe *you* could give *me* a clue."

"Carl, I'm not trying to bite your head—"

His brows shot up in exaggerated surprise. "Really? You could have fooled me."

"Come on. Let's not play these games."

"If *you're* playing a game, Sylvia, I can't help that."

"I'm not the one playing…" she began but realized the futility in trying to explain. She and Carl were in different worlds. Rather than the foot or two across their front seats, the gulf between them felt light years apart. "Just forget it."

Sylvia slumped back in her seat and stared out the sedan's windows at the parched hills. They were inland and heading north, somewhere between their home in Malibu and San Francisco.

If only her marriage was as clear as the stretch of road in front of them, but it was more like the 405 Freeway during rush hour.

Their latest snarl-up had been that morning as they packed for the trip. She had only wanted to know where they were going. Was that a capital offense? Otherwise, how would she know what to pack for the weekend? But Carl had refused to say, insisting it was a surprise.

Sure, a nice idea in theory, but how great could the surprise be if she had all the wrong clothes? What if he had planned a skiing trip, but she packed a bathing suit? What if she needed something dressy, but only had jeans? Didn't he see how ridiculous expecting her to prepare for a trip when she had no idea what they were doing was?

Of course, he had misunderstood, taken offense, and gotten defensive. And the rest of their prep had been in stony silence.

She now had a headache and a suitcase stuffed with a bizarre collection of clothes.

Would they ever untangle themselves from this mess? At this rate, how would they even survive a three-day weekend, which, whether they admitted it or not, was a last-ditch effort to save their marriage?

Massaging her throbbing temples, Sylvia closed her eyes. She appreciated Carl's effort. She really did. But she couldn't help but wonder if, after these last two years of being with each other nonstop during the pandemic, the way to salvage their relationship wasn't spending more time together, but less.

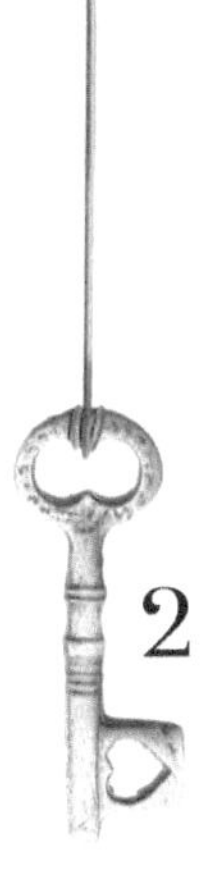

LET THE GAMES BEGIN

Another fifteen minutes passed in silence. The atmosphere in the car grew arctic.

Why hadn't she suggested dinner at Nobu? The restaurant was always a safe choice. It was popular, at the beach, close to their home, and open again now that social restrictions had lifted. Pricey enough to make the dinner special and loud enough that, if they weren't talking to each other, it wouldn't be as awkward.

But it was too late to change plans now. They were committed to this weekend away–good or bad.

She sighed. Wallowing would only make their time together worse. And who knew? Maybe they would turn off the highway and head to a seaside town. There were so many charming ones along the California coast. Once, they had enjoyed wasting full days together, strolling along main streets, stepping into galleries, window shopping, sharing a bottle of wine, walking hand in hand. Back then, intimacy had been easy and expected. Their connection as reliable as watching each sunset together and waking up each morning in the other's arms. The bittersweet memories felt like they were from another couple and another life. She guessed, in a way, they were.

But she and Carl would never have a chance for that kind of weekend—or life—again, if they weren't talking with one another. Pushing down her resentment, she mustered up the courage and determination to try again.

"Hey," she squeezed out.

"What?" Carl's voice was as edgy as she felt.

She sighed. "I'm sorry we argued. I know you put in a lot of effort toward making this special."

It took a long minute, but eventually, his expression softened. "Thanks."

She wanted to say something more to extend this fleeting moment of respite, but the unspoken words clogged her throat.

"It's not too much farther," he said, breaking the silence.

"It's inland?" She immediately regretted the note of disappointment she'd allowed to escape.

Carl stiffened. His mouth hardened back into the tight line of defensiveness, now its normal state. Of course, he knew her preferences all too well.

"That's fine—I just thought maybe we were going to cut over to the coast."

He frowned at her. "Why would I drive inland if we were going to the beach?"

"How should I know? You haven't told me anything."

"Right! Because I wanted this to be a suuurrrprrriiissse."

"Most surprises these days aren't pleasant ones," she muttered.

His scowl deepened. No selective deafness now. He had heard her comment loud and clear. "Great. That's just great. Why do you always pick everything apart? Can't we just relax and enjoy something for once?"

"That's what I'm trying to do!"

"Really? Interesting approach."

It was hopeless.

Sylvia turned away from him but couldn't bear staring out the window for another second. She pulled down the passenger visor and checked herself in the mirror. A tired version of her stared back. Her hair, which only a few years ago had been one of her favorite features, was now pulled back in a tight bun. Her workaround for not having seen a stylist in months. During the pandemic, she had stopped coloring it, but now that the salons were open, she just hadn't bothered to go back. Coarse gray had invaded the once-lustrous auburn. But the gray, or even extra wrinkles, weren't what bothered her. She still looked pretty good for a mom in her late forties with two kids. Her Peloton workouts helped. So did her DG shirt and Saint Laurent jeans. What concerned her was the weariness in her eyes, the tightness around her mouth, the seemingly ever-present frown. The lighthearted, vivacious woman she used to be was now trapped behind glass in hallway photos.

She was as fed-up as she was weary. Maybe she should call it quits. Stop trying and face facts. She and Carl didn't make each other happy anymore. Their marriage was a pathetic cliché—the empty nesters who had nothing in common. Their son and daughter were out of the house, living their own busy lives. At least she and Carl could feel good about that, and maybe that should be enough. Carl wasn't an attentive husband, but he was a great dad. She was grateful for that and for their shared devotion to family. But even his good parenting had its price.

Once they had kids, they had forgotten about each other. Not suddenly, but in increments. As a new mom, she had been so focused on her son, then, three years later on, her baby girl. Carl had asked her if she wanted to go out, but she hadn't wanted to leave them. He agreed and, over time, had stopped asking. Hundreds of insignificant choices added up to living more like roommates than lovers. Any vestige of their once warm and happy home had moved out with their kids.

Telling Martin and Grace they were separating wouldn't be easy, but their kids were young adults now and could handle it. Their oldest, Martin, was already making a name for himself in the law firm where he was interning, and Grace was doing well as a junior in college, enjoying her independence and studies. These days, Sylvia and Carl were lucky if their kids had time to call them each week. She didn't mind (too much). She was grateful they were healthy and leading fulfilling lives.

But what about her own? The now familiar tightness filled her chest. It came every time she landed upon the same, inevitable conclusion. Separation. She would do her best to make it amiable, even give Carl their home. She'd find an apartment. Start fresh in a new, smaller place. Her career as a marketing executive was no longer satisfying, but it paid well enough. Financial security wasn't keeping her in the marriage.

Sylva stole a glance at Carl, now humming a tuneless song. His once-chiseled face was a bit fuller and softer with age. He had gained a few pounds, especially over the last couple years while his gym had been closed. He was a few years older than her. Gray had just begun to peek out from the stubble on his cheeks, matching the start of salt-and-pepper hair. Like her, more wrinkles lined his eyes, but he was still a handsome man.

Separating would be one of the hardest things she ever did, but she could do it. She had the backbone.

A lack of courage or self-confidence wasn't what stopped her, or even a fear of being alone. In fact, she relished the moments when Carl was out of the house, which had been few and far between recently. She had never realized how helpful their separate professional lives had been until they had been forced to both work from home.

Maybe her hesitation was a fear of failure. Maybe simply inertia. Who knew?

The point was being halfway out of her marriage was tiring and painful.

"We're here," Carl announced, pulling her from her thoughts.

Sylvia refocused, noticing for the first time she had been pulling a loose thread from her cashmere sweater.

She looked up just in time to miss a flash of pink sign passing by. "Where?"

"Nope, still not saying." His voice was the lightest it had been all day. "You'll just have to see for yourself."

Carl was as quick to let go of his upset as he was to fall into it. She envied that. His boyish excitement lightened her own dark mood just a bit.

"Alright," she said aloud, though it was more to herself than to her husband. If she wasn't ready to have the "big talk" with him right now, then she should at least give them both this weekend as one last shot.

Whether Carl knew it or not, her twenty-fifth anniversary present to them both was to keep an open mind to the possibility that, perhaps, they could find a way through.

But for that possibility to become a reality…

They'd need nothing short of a miracle.

3

PRETTY (MUCH) IN PINK

arl maneuvered their Lexus onto a dusty, narrow incline. Old wooden fences lined both sides of the road. Some of the posts and boards were missing.

Sylvia stared at the scene in dismay. *Remember your anniversary present,* she reminded herself. *Keep an open mind.*

But what she saw decimated that idea, along with any chance of a pleasant weekend.

Rather than the cliffside home or elegant resort she was hoping for, the hotel coming into view looked like a Barbie playhouse on steroids.

The two-story hotel was pink. Pink exterior walls, pink pillars, pink balustrades on the second-floor walkways, even pink trash cans scattered around the (not surprisingly) empty parking lot that they pulled into.

Carl drove across the lot, choosing a parking spot close to a pink cement sidewalk (how do you color a sidewalk?) that led to a semicircular, two-story building, crowned with a pink spire. Over the front door was a matching pink sign.

Shutting off the engine, Carl gestured grandly to the sign. "Welcome to the Magdalene Inn!"

Her husband's sense of humor could devolve into pranks, but if this was a joke, it was in terrible taste.

"You're kidding, right?"

Carl didn't answer.

He didn't need to. Sylvia saw genuine hurt on his face, which was even worse. Her husband had actually chosen this spot for their anniversary. How could he possibly think she wanted to stay in a place like this? Was she that much of a stranger to him?

"We talked about this place. Don't you remember?"

Sylvia searched her memory for any random conversation when she might have been concussed, or in a fever, or held at gunpoint—because those were the only legitimate reasons she would ever be interested in this place.

Then it came to her. A couple months back, they had been channel surfing and stumbled upon a documentary on the kitschier side of California. Not surprisingly, the Magdalene Inn was featured.

"You wanted to know if it was still open," he pressed.

That was true. She had, but only because she couldn't believe a place so tacky could keep its doors open for so many years.

"That's what gave me the idea. If you were so interested, why not spend a weekend here? It sounded fun and, Lord knows, we could use some."

The note of reproach wasn't missed on her. Anger rose, replacing the disappointment.

Oblivious, he said, "I might have forgotten all about it, but an ad with a 50 percent discount for the inn appeared in my Facebook feed."

"So that's why you chose this place for our twenty-fifth anniversary—to save a few bucks?"

"Of course not! The ad showed up out of the blue. I took it as a sign. You're the one who's always saying, 'follow the Universe.'" He jabbed the air with invisible quotes.

"So, it's my fault we're in this dump! Why didn't you just ask me—"

"Yeah, that would have made for a great surprise, Sylvia."

"Oh, it's a surprise alright."

Carl threw up his hands. "I blew it again. No matter what I do, it's never good enough."

"That's not true."

"Really? Name one time you were happy about something I did in the last week." He held up a finger. "One time when you weren't annoyed or pointing out something I did wrong… just one."

Sylvia wanted to deny it, but when she thought about their recent week and how much they had fought, she couldn't recall a time they had been happy with one another.

When she didn't reply, he turned away from her. "I rest my case."

"I hate when you say that," she muttered.

"And I rest my case *again*!"

Why did she always end up the bad guy in their arguments? Was she just supposed to pretend she liked everything he did, no matter how wrong it was? She was so sick of compromising, of feeling like she was forever pulling the short straw.

Screw her anniversary gift. She gave up. She'd tell Carl right then and there she was moving out.

But instead, she screamed.

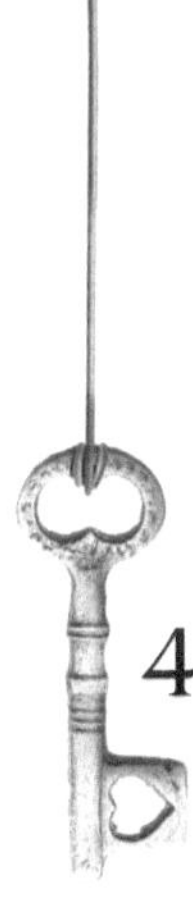

4

TWO VIEWS

"What the hell?" Carl glared at Sylvia.

Hand clasped over her mouth, she jerked her chin to the driver's window over his shoulder.

Carl turned and jerked back in his seat with a startled grunt.

Just inches from him, on the other side of the driver's side window, was the grinning, moon-shaped face of an elderly woman.

"Hello, you two!" the woman called out as if she were across the parking lot and not right next to them.

Where had she appeared from? Sylvia could swear she hadn't been there a second ago. The whole time they had been parked, she had been facing Carl, arguing with him, and the driver's side window was right behind him. Was she so crazed and caught up in their fight she hadn't noticed someone approaching? Sylvia shook her head. She really was losing it.

Carl clasped his chest. "Geez, you almost gave me a heart attack."

Sylvia didn't know if he was referring to her or the mystery woman outside their Lexus.

Totally oblivious, the woman winked coquettishly. "I know you two want your *alone time*, but I can guarantee we have better accommodations inside than in your car. Come on now, lovebirds. Let's get you checked in."

Sylvia winced at the term. They were about as close to lovebirds as two vultures.

"Now, don't be shy! You've paid good money for your stay. You should get started *staying*." The woman tittered at her own pun and gestured for Carl to unlock his door.

When he complied, she threw it open and reached in to give him a crushing hug, even though he was still buckled in.

He let out a strangled choke and looked at Sylvia in panic. She couldn't help but giggle. Their ridiculous embrace and his expression acted like cool water, extinguishing her anger. Following the woman's instructions, she climbed out of their car, grateful for the temporary reprieve.

Carl extracted himself from the woman's embrace and stepped out as well. He hurried away from her to the trunk, ostensibly to get their luggage, but probably as an excuse to put distance between himself and the crazed woman.

It was futile. She just followed him. "Goodness! Where are my manners? I'm Angie. I run the Magdalene with my husband, Harold, who's just inside. And you must be Mr. and Mrs. McAllister."

Carl nodded. "Yes, I'm Carl, and this is—"

"Your lovely wife, Sylvia." She regarded them both. "Oh yes, I know *all* about you two."

Sylvia frowned. Had Angie done a Google search on them? *Maybe she had*, she thought uneasily. They had nothing to hide, but it was creepy anyway.

"Let me say that Harold, I, and the entire staff of the Magdalene are overjoyed you're here! Your timing couldn't be more perfect!"

Sylvia knew Angie's enthusiasm was intended to be welcoming, but the creep-factor was just getting worse. Why was their timing perfect? She stole a glance at Carl, who lifted an eyebrow. He had felt it, too—the first time they had agreed on anything that week.

Before Carl could protest, Angie linked arms with him and half-dragged him to the other side of the car where Sylvia stood. Once there, she linked arms with her too. "Don't worry about your luggage. That'll be taken to your rooms."

"About that," Carl said, attempting and failing at extracting himself from the woman's grip. "We may not be able to stay."

Carl looked over Angie's head to Sylvia, raising his brows and glancing from her to Angie.

"That's right," Sylvia said, taking his lead. "There was a bit of a misunderstanding."

Angie let go of them to face her. "The Magdalene not to your liking, my dear?"

Heat rose in Sylvia's face. Of course, Angie had overheard their argument. She had been standing right outside their car. "It's not exactly that…"

"No need to pretend, dear. You're certainly not the first guest who has found the Magdalene a bit much." Angie gazed across the empty parking lot to the entrance, as if viewing the inn for the first time from their eyes. "You see a gaudy hotel with too many trimmings and too much pink…"

Sylvia groaned inwardly, thinking of the insults she had so casually thrown around. She glanced at Carl, who was busy studying the cracks in the bubblegum-colored sidewalk.

"But do you know what I see?" Angie gestured wide with her arms, her eyes shining. "All I see is wonder."

To her surprise, Sylvia didn't sense a shred of hurt or defensiveness coming from Angie.

But when she turned back to Sylvia, Angie's expression had lost its former silliness. She suddenly seemed more elegant and self-possessed, even a touch serious, as if an entirely different woman stood before her.

"That's the magic of it, my dear. You may see things very differently than I do… and both views are true… but it is a matter of choice." She pinned Sylvia with her gaze for a moment, then turned and marched up the sidewalk to the front door.

Sylvia was left a bit breathless and wondering what had just happened. Lost in her own questions, she didn't notice Carl had followed Angie until the two of them were at the front entrance with the door held open, waiting for her.

She hesitated. A part of her wanted to climb back in the car and have Carl handle it. The brief encounter with Angie had left her strangely off-balance, as if she were on the deck of a boat that had suddenly hit rough seas. She could use time alone to recover, but letting Carl handle their refund himself would be a mistake. He was such a pushover. He might just as likely be talked into staying.

Sylvia pulled her Prada handbag from the front seat, found her own set of keys at the bottom, and locked the car.

Once again, it was up to her to be the bad guy if they were going to get what they wanted.

As she walked past her husband and Angie to cross the threshold into the inn, she heard the proprietress say behind her, "The real question is: what view do *you* choose?"

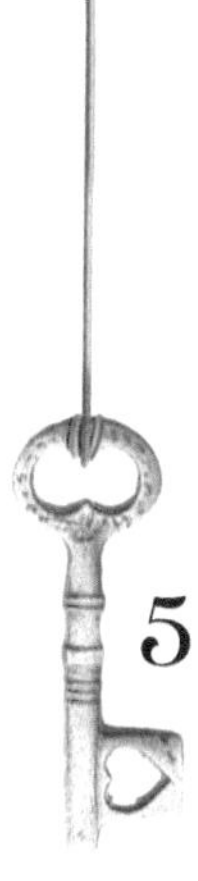

5

THE INVITATION

"You're here! Howdy-doody, folks!" a deep voice bellowed as soon as they entered the lobby of the Magdalene.

Sylvia froze just inside the entrance. If she had thought the outside had a lot of pink, it was understated compared to the lobby.

A fuchsia floral carpet stretched across the vast space, only interrupted by white floor vases containing towering arrangements of roses and peonies—both in the requisite shades of pink. Unlike the faux-Swiss exterior, the interior walls were built of thick Palos Verdes stone. Tucked against these walls were magenta sofas. Above them, the ceiling corners were crowded with Cupid statues. Each of the two or more dozen rotund baby angels was on its own little shelf. Some held tiny harps, others flowers, and still others miniature quivers of arrows. The only thing missing from the saccharine-sweet tableau was a Cupid with his arms stretched and a plaque saying, "I wuv you this much."

Not surprisingly, the lobby was empty.

Sylvia squinted against the cacophony of colors and decor, hoping to spot any other guests. An elderly man waved from across the room. But he was clearly not a guest because he stood behind a stone construction, presumably the front desk. A large, overly gilded mirror dominated the wall behind him.

Sylvia's nose wrinkled in disgust. She found decorative mirrors invasive. Who wanted to see themselves all the time? They made her self-conscious. But clearly, the white-haired man standing in front of the lobby mirror didn't share that problem. He seemed oblivious to the 360-degree view everyone was getting of him. His enormous belly strained the edges of his coral Hawaiian shirt.

"Greetings, dear guests, and felicitations!" He stepped out from the front desk and ambled over. The three walked forward to greet him. As soon as he reached them, he pumped Carl's hand, then turned to Sylvia, took her hand, and bowed over it like a courtier.

It was a little overdone, but the gallantry was surprisingly nice.

He straightened. "You must be Mr. and Mrs. McAllister. Aren't you both a sight for sore eyes—and here at just the right time too!"

There it was again. The over-enthusiasm that bordered on desperation.

Sylvia dismissed it. She was being paranoid. Of course, they were desperate. The lobby was empty. Any guests would be a sight for sore eyes. Any time would be the best time.

The man continued, placing a meaty hand on his chest. "I'm Harold, and you've already met my gorgeous wife, Angie."

Sylvia watched as Harold turned adoring eyes to his wife, who blushed like a young teen. Clearly, the couple had been together for years, and yet somehow, they had found a way to not only stay together but still be in love with one other. A fleeting pang of jealousy passed through her.

Angie reached out and took Harold's hand. It was such a small gesture, but as foreign and faraway to Sylvia as a distant planet.

Embarrassed to feel moisture in her eyes, she turned away from the small intimacy and got busy pretending to search for something in her purse.

Carl cleared his throat. "It's nice to meet you, Harold. Both you and Angie. But I'm afraid to say Sylvia and I need to cancel our reservation."

Angie and Harold exchanged worried glances.

"We're not trying to get out of paying any cancellation fees," Carl hurried on.

Sylvia swiped at her eyes with a crumpled tissue. "We understand this is last-minute. We're willing to pay whatever Carl agreed to in the contract."

In fact, she hoped there was a cancellation fee. Paying it would help get rid of the guilt pricking her. It felt foolish to admit, but she didn't want to let them down. Angie and Harold weren't bad people. Unconventional and eccentric, certainly, but they came from a different generation, one that was more sentimental—perhaps even naive—and far less cynical. If the Cupids were any indication, their hearts seemed to be in the right place. They were doing their best to create a romantic place for their guests. It wasn't their fault their tastes were diametrically opposed to hers. She wished a few statuettes were the only thing she and Carl needed to regain their lost romance.

"Heavens, that's very generous but not at all necessary," Harold said. "The Magdalene never charges a cancellation fee."

"Really? That's… unique." Sylvia wondered how in the world their business survived. One of her current campaigns was promoting a boutique hotel in Beverly Hills, and it wasn't her first foray into the hospitality industry. Most hotels operated with low profit margins, and the pandemic had forced many to close their doors. Now that travel was open again, cancellation fees were critical to protect against lost revenues due to last-minute changes. The same kind of changes she and Carl were requesting, Sylvia realized with another pang of regret.

She pushed the emotion aside. No, she would not stay and ruin her weekend just because she felt guilty. They offered to pay a cancellation fee, and the couple had refused, despite their desperate need for guests. Harold and Angie were professionals and had managed to keep their business afloat, even during the last two years. They knew what they were doing.

"We decided a long time ago that we were never going to force anyone to stay here. It would go against the very spirit of this place and its namesake. She's the patron saint of anyone who, in any way, feels themselves to be trapped," Angie said.

Harold's face turned solemn. "It's very important you stay at the Magdalene of your own volition."

There it was again. That same strange, sudden gravity she had felt from Angie outside.

No one spoke for an awkward moment.

Then Angie broke the silence by laughing. "Besides, we don't need a cancellation policy because nobody cancels!"

Sylvia frowned. "But outside, you said we weren't the first ones—"

"Who didn't find the Magdalene to their liking?" Angie finished. "True, but eventually, everyone stays."

She and Carl exchanged sidelong looks.

"Welcome to the Hotel California," Carl sang under his breath.

Sylvia coughed to suppress a giggle.

Catching their exchange, Harold raised a hand. "They *choose* to stay because they want to."

"Quite right, my love," Angie said, "especially after they hear about our special offer."

Inwardly, Sylvia rolled her eyes. Of course… the catch.

As if reading her mind, Angie said, "No catch. Just an invitation."

"Invitation?" Carl asked before Sylvia could stop him.

"Indeed." Harold nodded. "One which, if you choose to accept, will change your life."

6

THE GUARANTEE

"Change our lives? How?" Carl asked.

Here we go, Sylvia thought, inwardly rolling her eyes. She hated to be cynical, but eighteen years overseeing marketing campaigns did that to a person. Though she had to hand it to Angie and Harold. They were good. The "kindly old couple" act had won her over, and even made her feel guilty. In just a few minutes, the pair had successfully taken down her and Carl's defenses and opened them up for the real sale. She wondered what it would be. The amount of time both had spent—it couldn't just be for the meager price of a weekend. Maybe they sold timeshares. Now, that made more sense. Those cost $20,000 to $40,000 these days. Unfortunately, she had caught on too late. Her husband, who was unfamiliar with these types of marketing ploys, had fallen for their trap.

"It will change the very nature of your relationship," Harold said.

"Really? In what way?" Sylvia couldn't keep the skepticism from her tone.

Angie turned to her. "In the way you're secretly hoping it will, Sylvia. You and Carl will once again experience the love that has eluded you for years."

Sylvia jerked back as if she had been slapped.

"You sure don't pull punches," Carl snapped.

He held out a steadying hand to Sylvia, which she automatically refused, then realized how that, too, must have appeared. Were their problems so obvious to everyone?

Her eyes strayed to the large, framed mirror behind the front desk, standing like a sentinel of the lobby. Now that they had moved farther into the room, it reflected all four of them. Two couples who were worlds apart. Howard and Angie were smiling, standing close together, holding hands. Sylvia was embarrassed to see how obvious her and Carl's tension with one another was. Her rigid posture. Carl's raised shoulders. The distance between them. Immediately, she dropped her arms, which had been crossed over her chest, but it made little difference. Their body language telegraphed their problems in a dozen different ways.

"I'm sorry. That was rather direct, wasn't it?" Angie looked to Carl and then to Sylvia. "But you did ask. If I've misspoken…"

Neither of them answered.

"You're certainly not alone," Angie said more gently.

Anger rose inside of Sylvia. This had gone too far. Throwing their failed marriage in their faces to get a sale, no matter how big, was way out of line.

"How can you promise anything?" Carl asked.

"They can't." Sylvia pulled on her husband's arm. "Let's get out of here."

"Actually, we can," Harold said. "If you stay here at the Magdalene, we guarantee your marriage will be significantly improved."

"Or what? We get our deposit back?" Sylvia shot back. "That means nothing to us." And it certainly didn't justify being insulted and submitted to their manipulation.

"We know that your time is much more valuable than that, which is why we'll do one better," Harold said.

This couple was too much. She knew what "one better" was. In marketing it was called "the double guarantee." Give potential customers double their money back if they're not satisfied. Surprisingly, it wasn't a risky tactic. Most people never asked for a refund, and it often closed the sale.

She held up a hand. "Getting double our money back doesn't get our time back."

Harold nodded. "You're right, Sylvia. It doesn't. That's why we wouldn't dream of offering you such a paltry amount. As I said before, your time is much more valuable. It's clear you are a successful couple…"

"*Financially* speaking," Angie said.

Sylvia flushed again. She gripped Carl's arm tighter.

"Money isn't the issue for you," Harold said. "But experience is. That's why we're giving an experience guarantee. If your marriage isn't improved by the end of your stay here at the Magdalene, we will provide you with *any* anniversary trip of your choosing. If you want to stay in an Italian castle, a Greek island, the Taj Mahal—"

"No one can stay in the Taj Mahal," Sylvia said.

Angie smiled. "You'd be surprised at our connections."

"You'll make this guarantee in writing?" Carl asked.

"It's our pleasure." Harold headed over to the front desk, waving for them to join him. He pulled out a printed piece of paper from a drawer, signed his name with a flourish, and then handed it to them.

Both Sylvia and Harold read what was written there:

The Magdalene Inn guarantees that Carl and Sylvia McAllister's marriage will significantly improve by the end of their stay, per their verbal or written acknowledgement. If based upon the McAllisters' own assessment, they do not experience a significant improvement in their relationship, the

Magdalene Inn guarantees that they will book a replacement anniversary trip at the location of the McAllisters' choice. All expenses paid. No location, timing, or cost limits.

Whistling under his breath, Carl turned to Sylvia. "Syl, what do you think?"

"Give us a minute." Sylvia took the paper and headed over to the nearest couch. Carl followed. She read then reread the short contract. Finally, she looked up at him, admitting, "This is the craziest guarantee I've ever seen."

"But is it binding?"

She stared down at the little paragraph holding the biggest promise she had ever run across in all her years in marketing. "I guess it is. As long as we also sign and date it."

He took the contract from her and set it down before facing her. "What do you want to do?"

The problem was she didn't know. Actually, that wasn't true. Part of her wanted to leave. To get out—and quick—before she was made an even bigger fool. The marketing exec duped by two senior citizens.

But another part of her was curious to play this through. What if there was even a slim chance of what Angie and Harold claimed? What if she and Carl had been given a "get out of jail free" card? Was it worth the risk to find out?

She chewed on a thumbnail. She hated being so indecisive. In her career, she made dozens of tough choices every day without a second thought.

Frustrated, she shrugged. "I don't know. What do you think is best?"

He shook his head. "No, sorry. This is your call, Syl. I'm the one who got us into this mess. And if you want to walk away right now, I'm totally fine with your choice."

Whatever their decision, she appreciated the way Carl acknowledged his part in the fiasco. And she agreed with him: this was her decision to make. But did it have to be? Somehow, it felt too big, too critical, to make on her own.

Sylvia followed his gaze down to the paper between them on the couch, a tenuous bridge connecting them. Was it too late to cross it to a new future?

"Worst case, we walk away with an amazing trip," he said.

She couldn't argue. A trip of their choosing anywhere in the world with no time or budget limits—who ever got a deal like that? Despite her well-developed cynicism, she couldn't deny the tiny flame of hope their outlandish offer lit inside her. How could this couple offer this huge of a guarantee without being sure of the outcome? Unlike the "double guarantee" tactic, this offer was so outrageous no one in their right mind would pass it by. In fact, it might work as a disincentive. If this were offered to all the Magdalene guests, some couples might purposely spoil their weekend just to claim the all-expense-paid trip. Which raised the obvious question: what if their claim wasn't a lie? What if they really could help?

She didn't want to hope. Hope just led to disappointment.

And what about your promise to keep an open mind? her inner voice countered.

Sylvia realized her hands were sweaty. She wiped them on her jeans and faced her husband. "Carl, this can't just be my choice. This feels far too important for me to make the call alone."

He nodded and lapsed into silence. After several moments, he said, "I don't believe for one minute they can guarantee our marriage will be better."

She bit her lip, looking down. He was only being honest, but hearing Carl admit defeat out loud hurt more than she expected.

But then he took her hand. It was such a small gesture, but it meant a lot.

"Hear me out," he said. "I don't believe they can guarantee it, but I *want* to believe."

Peering back up at him, she saw a mixture of regret and anxiousness. "What about you?"

To her surprise, she answered without hesitating, "I do too."

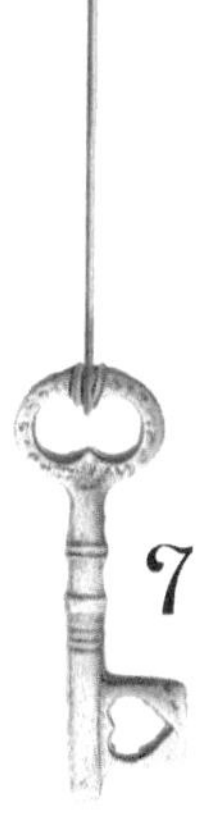

THE BRIDGE BETWEEN THEN AND NOW

ylvia and Carl followed their hosts, who had been "over the moon" to hear they were going to stay and had insisted on escorting them to their room. What hotel owners ever took this level of care with their guests, unless they were celebrities? Another oddity, but Sylvia was getting used to everything being strange at the Magdalene.

They headed down a corridor wallpapered in a soft rose print—an understated relief to the gaudiness of the lobby—the sound of their footfalls absorbed in the thick matching carpet.

Sylvia recognized this hall, showcased in the documentary she and Carl had watched. Each door they passed had a polished brass plaque. Sylvia read them as they walked by—*The Scarlett & Rhett Room…The Elizabeth & Darcy Room…The Tarzan & Jane Room.*

The video segment had mentioned these same rooms in a photo montage but hadn't included any actual video footage. Why didn't they? Perhaps the inn's current issue with low occupancy was due to the pandemic, and the rooms had been filled at the time of the filming.

But even with low occupancy, there should be some other guests.

Since their arrival, she hadn't seen anyone other than Harold and Angie. Not even another staff member. Even small boutique hotels had bellhops or housekeepers running around, and inevitably, a few guests lounging in the lobby.

But there was no one.

Stranger still, the hall was totally silent, with none of the typical sounds one would expect: bits of conversation, an ice machine running, the muffled sounds of a TV as they passed by a room. Not even a discarded room service tray waited to be picked up in the hall.

Nothing.

Getting more and more anxious, Sylvia tightened her grip on her purse with their guarantee signed, dated, and tucked safely inside.

She wished her concern had to do with Angie and Harold reneging on their promise.

But her worry was the exact opposite.

Their two hosts were totally sincere about overhauling Carl's and her marriage, but what lengths were they willing to go?

What had she and Carl gotten themselves into?

"So how does this work?" she asked, flinching at how strident her own voice sounded in the tomb-like silence of the hall. She added more quietly, "I mean, do we have to take classes or—?"

"This isn't therapy, is it?" Carl blurted. "Because I didn't agree to that."

Their one attempt at seeing a therapist had ended in disaster. Granted, they had gone to only part of the first session. After thirty minutes, Carl stormed out, accusing both her and the therapist of ganging up on him. In hindsight, she shouldn't have found the therapist on her own. Maybe if Carl had helped her select a couples counselor, he would have been more open to it. But who knew? No matter what they tried, they just couldn't get it right.

So how in the world could staying a few days in this inn make any difference?

"Therapy? No, no, nothing like that," Harold said as he turned left and headed down another empty hallway. "But how does it work? Gosh, what a great question. I can't say, exactly. Angie, darlin', can you?"

Taking his wife's hand, he made a quick right and headed down yet another abandoned corridor. The place was a labyrinth.

"What I can say is that there are lessons, but no classes," Angie said enigmatically.

The two chuckled together.

Sylvia's jaw tightened at their private joke. "What's that supposed to mean?"

Behind her, Carl laid a hand on her shoulder. His way to tell her to calm down. She wriggled free. His attempts to control her only made her more upset.

Harold and Angie halted at the end of the corridor in front of a single, closed door.

Angie turned to face them both. "Not to worry. You won't be stuck in some boring lecture or classroom."

"Nothing boring about it," Harold said.

"Which doesn't answer my question," Sylvia said. "What specifically can we expect?"

"Do you know the physiological difference between fear and excitement?" Angie asked, but she didn't wait for a response. "It's breath. Isn't that interesting? The only difference between feeling anxious or excited is simply breathing."

Angie took in a deep breath, and Carl automatically followed suit.

But Sylvia refused to follow Angie blindly, especially given the woman's evasiveness. Her hand gripped her purse. One more quip and she would rip up the contract and hand it back to them in pieces—all-expenses-paid trip or not. She would not be made a fool.

As if hearing her, Angie shook her head. "We're not trying to be vague, Sylvia. The Magdalene's like electricity. We don't know how it works, but that doesn't stop us from using it. Do you see?"

No, she didn't, and she sure wasn't going to put her faith in some mysterious, invisible process. "That makes no sense."

Shrugging, Harold cracked open the closed door. "Does life make sense? Does anything make sense for that matter?"

Angie nodded. "But there is one thing I can tell you both. It's absolutely your choice. Stay or go. Keep things the same or…" She gestured to the door. "Enter the possibility of a whole new beginning!"

In front of them on the partially open oak door was a shiny brass plaque: *The Romeo & Juliet Room.*

CROSSING THE THRESHOLD

Seriously? Could there be anything more cliché? The thought of them staying in an homage to young love was intolerable. She and Carl only had one thing in common with Romeo and Juliet: both of their relationships were tragedies.

She turned to Carl. "You reserved *this* room?"

He shook his head. "No! I had no idea."

His look of repugnance should have reassured her, but for some reason, it just made her more annoyed. Couldn't she get a break? Couldn't one thing be smooth or easy? She felt like the brunt of a cosmic joke.

Angie stepped in. "We booked it on your behalf. Well, not *us* exactly, the inn's questionnaire."

Pulled out of her own musings, Sylvia frowned. "Questionnaire?"

Carl cleared his throat. "Uh…they sent us a questionnaire, which I filled out." Before she could protest, he rushed on. "I couldn't show it to you without spoiling the surprise."

Right. The great surprise. So, Carl had answered the questions himself. A terrible thought struck her. "What kind of questions?"

Carl's cheeks reddened as Angie piped in, "About your relationship. Its strengths and opportunities for growth… that sort of thing."

Just when she thought it couldn't get worse. Now complete strangers had been let in on their marital problems? No wonder Angie and Harold had seemed to know a lot about them! She could only imagine Carl's responses.

Angie beamed at them. "You got matched to this room based on your responses."

"*I* didn't have any responses." Sylvia glowered at Carl.

Angie waved a hand dismissively. "Don't worry. It's not mandatory. One partner's responses will do. The Magdalene always knows the perfect room."

"Great," Carl said, clearly in a hurry to move off the topic. "Then what's next?"

"Just step on in. Your bags are already inside," Harold said. "And there should be a lovely bottle of wine waiting for you. On the house… or *on the Inn* I should say!"

Both he and Angie laughed.

"Thanks." Carl stepped in front of the couple, pushing the door more open.

Sylvia tried to peer around him to get a glimpse of the room, but Carl's bulky frame blocked the view. She hesitated. This was her chance. If she didn't want to go through with it, she should speak up now and call it off. But was that what she wanted? Despite how utterly irritating her hosts were, a part of her yearned for everything Harold and Angie offered. Hadn't she told herself a thousand times how much she wanted their relationship to get better?

"Sylvia?" Carl asked as the three of them looked at her expectantly.

What she saw in her husband's expression surprised her.

It was hope. Not much. Just a tiny spark of it, flickering amidst the weariness and anxiety.

But it was there, and she hadn't seen it for a very long time.

Before she could second guess anymore, she answered him, "I'm coming."

Whether good or bad, at least she had decided. And, really, how bad could it be?

Sylvia moved past Carl, stepping through the open door…

Into sudden darkness.

9

THE ROMEO & JULIET ROOM

Something caught Sylvia's heel, and she stumbled forward, instinctively bracing with her hands. She fell against the wall. Its surface was rough, cold, and almost wet to the touch. Recoiling, she cursed the bellhop who had dropped off their luggage without bothering to turn on a light.

Then something occurred to her that made her breath catch. How could a bellhop have dropped off their bags? They hadn't taken them from the trunk of their car, and no valet took their keys.

Once again, as if reading her mind, Angie's voice sang out from the hallway, "Remember to use the key." Her voice sounded strangely faraway.

Something felt very wrong. Sylvia turned to step back into the hall, but Carl closed the door behind them before she could.

"What are you doing? Open the door."

"I can't see anything," his voice answered from the dark.

"So, open the door. It'll give us enough light to find a wall switch."

She heard some muffled thuds, then his voice saying, "I can't find the doorknob."

"Oh, for heaven's sake," she grumbled and pushed past him to the door. But when she reached out, all she felt was the same rough surface of stone. The door to their room was oak. She was sure of it. Somehow, both she and Carl had gotten turned around. She took a couple steps in both directions, holding out her hands, trying to locate the smooth surface of the door and access to the outside hall and light, but she came across yet more stone. Eventually, she gave up. "I can't find it either."

"No problem. I've got something."

A moment later, a small light appeared, a disposable cigarette lighter. Its tiny flame illuminated Carl's face from below, creating a ghoulish cast.

It didn't help the churning in her stomach. "You look like a character in a haunted house."

He scowled, making him seem even more macabre.

"Lift it higher so we can find the door."

When he obliged, a bit more of the space came into view, but no door.

"I don't get it. It should be right there." Carl gestured to the wall with the hand holding the lighter. As he moved about, the flame fluttered.

"Why do you have a lighter? You gave up cigarettes years ago."

He turned away, ostensibly to search for either the door or a light switch, but not before a sheepish expression crossed his face.

"You haven't started back again, have you?"

"There has to be a light somewhere." Avoiding her question, he moved away from her, deeper into the room.

Sylvia followed, not wanting to be left alone in the dark. She shivered at the chill in the room. "I hope the light switch is next to the thermostat."

"Yeah, it's freezing in here," Carl said. "Hold on, I think I've found something."

Sylvia waited. With his back to her, she couldn't see what Carl was doing. Suddenly, warm light filled the space.

Carl held up a lit candle, a triumphant grin on his face.

"Where did you find it?" she asked, taking it.

"Right here." He indicated a table behind him. On it were several large candelabras set every few feet. Carl lit the rest of the candles in the two nearest him.

The extra light illuminated their surroundings.

Sylvia gasped. They weren't in just a hotel room. The suite was gargantuan. The entire first floor of their home could have fit inside.

"Carl, look at this place!"

They stood at the far end of a vast, rectangular room. All four walls were lined with tapestries.

"It's a great hall," Carl said in awe.

He was right to be. It was an incredible replica.

During their trips to Europe, she and Carl had toured real great halls, and they often were locations of the period movies she loved to watch.

Running the room's length on both sides were rough-hewn tables, butted up end to end. Both sets stopped at a raised platform, or dais, which had another table set with its own unlit candelabra, decanter, and goblets. If memory served, the dais ensured the lords, ladies, and their honored guests were "heads and shoulders above the rest" when they were dining.

Carl whistled softly. "I can't even imagine how much it cost to build this. Do you think all the rooms here are as big?"

"How could they be? The documentary we watched said the Magdalene had over a hundred rooms. It would have to be blocks long."

She turned slowly, taking in more of the vast room. The tapestry nearest them was of a woman and unicorn, a classic motif she had seen in various museums and castles. But this hanging was brightly colored, not at all like the faded ones she had viewed. The woman's gown was a vivid emerald, her hair a strawberry blonde. Sylvia could see the separate strands of red and gold in the woman's hair. One hand rested on the back of the unicorn. The other held a red egg.

Sylvia reached out to touch the corner. The tapestry itself was thick, made up of thousands of individual threads. Some felt like wool. Others like silk. And there were sharp threads, she guessed metallic. When she held her candle closer to the hanging, gold threads, woven as accents, glinted. Had it been real, this single tapestry would be worth a fortune. She pulled back her candle, not wanting the flame to get too close. Even as reproductions, these tapestries had to be quite expensive.

Somehow, the sight of the beautiful tapestry with its unicorn and maiden calmed her. She turned to Carl. "Okay, I admit—I'm glad we took Angie and Harold up on their offer and got this room. Romeo and Juliet seemed so trite and tacky out in the hall, but now that we're inside… well… it's incredible."

The candlelight caught Carl's self-satisfied smile. "I'm glad you're happy about it."

A corner of her mouth lifted. "Don't look so smug, McAllister."

"It's nice to be the king."

Rolling her eyes, she headed down the length of the tables, lighting the other candles along the way. The extra light further brightened the room, revealing rushes covering the floor—what she had tripped on earlier. They gave off a pleasant, earthy scent as she walked on them.

She climbed the few steps up to the dais, calling over her shoulder, "I think I've found the wine."

"Good! I could use it!"

As Carl joined her on the dais, she pulled out the cork from the vintage decanter. She filled two goblets, handing one over. She took a sip, but immediately spat it back into her glass. "Eww. Has this turned?"

Carl took a tentative sip and shook his head. "I don't think so, but it's not great. Kind of syrupy and sweet. I taste raisins."

"Too bad." She set down the goblet.

"No matter. We can get another bottle at dinner." He looked around, then pointed. "There's the door! How did we get so turned around?"

The heavy wood door was closed and at the far end of the room, on the opposite side from where she swore they had entered. Sylvia frowned. Her sense of direction was worse than she thought.

Apparently, Carl was thinking the same thing. "I must be getting old. I normally know where I am."

Just then, the door flew open. A blonde teenager bounced out from behind it and scampered into the room, skidding to a halt when she saw them.

"You're here." She dropped into a curtsy before popping back up. "Hi. I'm Juliet."

10

FOR NEVER WAS A STORY OF MORE WOE...

The gossamer girl before them was petite with high cheekbones, an elfin nose, and rosebud lips. She pulled a scarf from around her neck and waved it like a flag. "Welcome to my home. Did you find the wine? Any left?"

The girl scampered across the room, leapt onto the platform, and helped herself.

"Now wait a minute," Sylvia called after her. The girl couldn't be older than sixteen. A mental image appeared of Carl and her charged with furnishing alcohol to a minor.

Carl clapped once. "Hey, stop that!"

Ignoring them both, the girl downed the contents of the goblet, wiped her mouth with the back of her hand, jumped off the dais, and skipped back over to them.

"Juliet Montague." She stuck out the same hand, still wet.

Nothing if not fastidious, Carl only grimaced at the proffered hand. "I'm Carl, and this is my wife, Sylvia."

Sylvia stepped forward to shake Juliet's hand. "Juliet of *Romeo and Juliet?*" Maybe the girl was a drama student. She could imagine a summer job like that would be a lot of fun, but this girl could use more acting lessons. Her language, mannerisms, and outfit were modern, rather than the fifteenth century when the play was supposed to take place. Sylvia was no literary scholar, but she knew a bit about Shakespeare from films and plays. Given the lengths and expense Angie and Harold had invested to reproduce the Capulets' castle, this girl would have surely been issued the correct costume. But instead of a floor-length gown, she wore an anachronistic pair of loose, dove-gray pants and a black shirt, cinched awkwardly at the waist with what appeared to be a knotted pair of knee socks.

"OMG!" Juliet pointed to Sylvia's feet. "Are those Ferragamos? Can I try them on? I think we're the same size!"

Juliet kicked off her pair of cream-colored mule pumps. The beautiful, studded shoes skidded a few feet across the floor, then came to rest.

Sylvia pursed her lips. Those were $900 Valentino Garavanis, and the girl had treated them like flip-flops. Sylvia knew the shoes and their cost because she had packed the same type for this weekend trip. Her eyes narrowed as she recognized the Hermès scarf and the Oscar de la Renta blouse. "Are those my clothes?"

"Are they? Thank you! I *love* them!" Juliet said, stroking the silk of the blouse as she might a cat.

"But I didn't—"

"Are these swords?" Juliet stretched the scarf to get a better look at the navy, silver, and ivory pattern. "Romeo is going to go wild!"

"Juliet!" a male voice bellowed as if on cue. A moment later, a handsome young man in a hose and doublet stormed through the door. His dark brows were knit together in a scowl, and his already tanned skin was flushed red with anger. "I am going to kill Tybalt! This time he has gone too—oh, good morrow." The young man stopped short when he saw Sylvia and Carl. He recovered quickly, sweeping into a courtly bow.

"Ro-Ro, come meet our new friends," Juliet sang out sweetly.

The young man hurried over. All traces of his earlier upset had vanished, replaced with eager attentiveness. "Lord and Lady McAllister, I presume? You are most welcome to our home."

Bemused, Sylvia regarded him. At least he was trying to stay in character, though his Old English seemed a bit spotty.

"I trust that my only love has seen to thine every comfort?"

"Including getting started on our unpacking," Sylvia said, one brow arching.

Romeo eyed Juliet's outfit and wagged a finger. "Sweeting, did we not agree? No pilfering of our guests' belongings."

She pouted prettily. "Don't scold, Ro-Ro. I wouldn't have to if you would just get me something new every once in a while."

He threw up both arms. "Hast thou forgotten thy Lululemon leggings? They cost a king's ransom!"

She sniffed. "That was last week."

"Excuse me," Carl said, holding up a hand. "But my wife and I have been on the road for a while. Would you mind telling us where our room is? We would like to get settled."

"And get my clothes back," Sylvia added.

Reddening, Romeo shot a withering glance at Juliet, who stuck her tongue out at him.

The two were better at emulating a real married couple than playing the world's most ardent lovers.

Ignoring Juliet, Romeo extended his arm gallantly to Sylvia. "My lady?"

Sylvia took his arm. Romeo escorted her through the door into a low-ceilinged corridor, lit with flaming wall sconces. Carl and Juliet followed closely behind.

"So how long have you worked for Angie and Harold?" Sylvia asked, trying to make conversation as they strolled past a couple of closed doors. Did those lead to other guest suites? Maybe they shared the space. That would certainly make more sense.

Romeo bristled. "I do not work for anyone."

Juliet cleared her throat. When Sylvia turned around, the girl grimaced, shaking her head.

Unfortunately, the warning came too late.

"I am the master and lord of this household," Romeo stated, a little too loudly.

"Indeed, you are, my love," Juliet placated as she squeezed past. She pulled an ornate iron key from her pants pocket and hurriedly inserted it into a door near the end of the corridor.

"But isn't this Lord and Lady Capulet's castle?" Carl protested.

Typical of her husband to be fixated on the facts and oblivious to the social cues.

"Perhaps this is another castle, Carl."

"No, I've seen the movie. There's only one castle, and it's owned by Lord and Lady Capulet. Your parents," Carl said, turning to Juliet, who rolled her eyes.

"I and my good wife are lord and lady of this house." Romeo's voice turned chilly. He moved away from Sylvia to stand by Juliet's side. "This home and its lands were part of Juliet's dowry."

"It's *our* little slice of heaven." Juliet's warning expression belied the sweetness of her tone.

"Hold on a minute. You're saying you and Juliet are married?" Carl glanced over to Sylvia.

As lost as he was, she shrugged. They had both seen the play several times, as well as all the movies. And one thing was certain: they all ended the same, and it sure wasn't with a wedding scene.

Carl held up a hand. "Call me old-fashioned, but isn't that a bit sacrilegious? We are talking Shakespeare here."

Juliet's eyes flashed. "Only if you want us to blindly follow a two-bit bully who's more concerned with selling tickets than the impact of his words. How dare he sentence us to death when our only crime was to love one another!"

"Now, dearest, do not upset yourself," Romeo said, which to Sylvia was a bit like the pot calling the kettle black, but she refrained from saying as much.

Juliet whirled on Romeo. "Pray, tell me. How can I not? The man is a festering boil, a smooth-tongued toad. His vile words hath struck us dead a thousand times or more! A pox on him and his poisoned pen!"

Odd how the girl's language shifted as she grew more upset. Juliet no longer sounded like a ditzy Valley girl. She seemed realer, better resembling her namesake. And Sylvia could swear her anger was no act.

Clearly, something more was going on here than just a pair of high schoolers playing their parts, and Sylvia wanted to get to the bottom of it. "You know, I always hated that ending."

Juliet's outburst stopped immediately, her doe-like eyes opening even bigger. "You do?"

"I think everybody does."

Juliet threw up her hands. "Have I not said as much! Pray, speak on, gentle friend."

"No one wanted you to die. Either of you," Sylvia said, gesturing to her and Romeo.

"Thank you!" Juliet clasped Sylvia's hand in both of her own. "And that is exactly why I rewrote our story!"

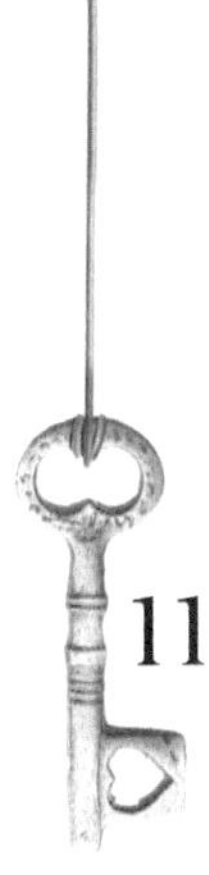

11

THE RIGHT TO REWRITE

Carl snorted. "You rewrote *Romeo and Juliet*? The play?"

Juliet's pert chin rose. "It's *our* lives after all. We should have the right to change it."

"Rewrite Shakespeare?" Carl scoffed. "The greatest playwright in history?"

"Carl," Sylvia warned.

Juliet flushed with anger.

Romeo jumped in, "Dearest…" He placed a hand on Juliet's arm, which she shrugged off.

Sylvia noted Romeo's attempt to "calm down" Juliet was received just as poorly as Carl's when she was angry.

Romeo cast a pleading glance in their direction. "My lord and his lady are in need of rest."

"We could use some." Carl moved closer to the door. "Sylvia? Why don't we get settled?"

Sylvia regarded her husband. Now that he had insulted their hosts, he was sensitive to social cues.

Hastily, Romeo leaned around Juliet to open the door. He pulled the key from the lock and handed it to Carl.

"Thank you," Carl said.

Juliet made no move to step aside.

"Thank you… both?" Carl offered, but Juliet remained in front of the door. Instead, she purposefully looked away from Carl and up to the ceiling.

Everyone lapsed into an uncomfortable silence. Romeo picked invisible lint from his doublet, and Carl glanced at Sylvia beseechingly.

Naturally, it was up to her to make amends. On the other hand, it did give her another opportunity to find out what was going on. Sylvia stepped forward. "I'm glad you rewrote the ending. I'm sure it's even better than the original."

Juliet nodded. "Thank you. It is," she said primly, but the compliment had its intended effect. Pacified, Juliet's dour expression evaporated like so many clouds, replaced by her sunnier disposition. She gave Sylvia a conspiratorial smile as she pulled her aside. "Would you like to know what I did? I can show you. It was quite simple."

Finally. Sylvia leaned forward to whisper, "I'd love to see."

Suddenly, Carl was next to them. "Our hosts have taken up enough of their time with us. Let's not keep them from their other duties." He pulled her through the door, shutting it in Juliet's face.

Sylvia rounded on him. "What was that about?"

Carl pointed to the door. "That girl is deranged."

"Please."

"She could be dangerous."

"How? She's going to strangle you with my Hermès scarf?"

Harrumphing, Carl moved Sylvia aside so he could lock the door from within.

"Aren't you even a little curious about what's going on here? Did you notice that when she got angry, Juliet's language changed? And what was all that about rewriting Shakespeare?"

"All I know is that every person we've met in this place is certifiable." Carl held up the key. "But we now have a locked door between them and us, so maybe, just maybe, we can relax. Can we try to do that for a few minutes, please?"

"Okay, I'll back off." Sylvia could see he needed the reprieve. Come to think of it, so did she. The day had been stressful enough, and they had the whole weekend to figure out what was going on.

Carl crossed and dropped onto the bed, sinking a few inches into its thick coverlet. "They may be crazy, but I can't fault their accommodations."

"It's even more gorgeous than the banquet hall," she said, taking in their suite.

Though it was much smaller, their bedroom could have been plucked from a fairy tale. The massive four-poster bed was ornately carved. The bed hangings and duvet were a surprising royal blue, rather than pink, velvet with elaborate embroidery. A carved oak chest rested at the foot of the bed. Across from the bed was a fireplace with a crackling log fire. Another set of carved pieces, a medieval vanity and chair, were tucked inside an alcove across the room. On the chair was her overnight case, open with her once carefully packed clothes spilling from it.

Annoyed, she eyed the pilfered luggage. A thought suddenly occurred to her. "Did you give Angie or Harold our car keys?"

Carl stretched like a cat. "This bed is amazing. We should find out what kind it is and get one."

"That girl better give me my clothes back."

"I hope she takes her time. I'd like to enjoy a few minutes of peace."

Sylvia straightened her clothes, throwing a heavier pashmina around her shoulders, and moved to the lit fireplace, rubbing her hands in front of the fire.

Unexpectedly, Carl joined her. He stood with his back to the blaze, then turned to face it. "This feels good."

It felt heavenly. As the warmth seeped in, her tension slowly slipped away. Sylvia took a deep breath, then let it out.

"Good idea." Carl shut his eyes, inhaling, and exhaling.

They stood shoulder to shoulder, enjoying the fire. After the previous craziness, she had to admit Carl was right. A moment of quiet was nice. The only sound was the crackling and popping of the logs. It reminded her of how they used to be. Easy. Relaxed. She stole a glance at Carl. His eyes were still closed, and a small, contented smile touched his face, which made her smile too. Besides passing one another in the hall, they hadn't been this close in a while.

Their hands were just inches away from one another. Should she take his? They had held hands thousands of times. But reaching for his hand, after they had been so distant, felt vulnerable… and tempting. Was this what Angie and Harold had meant when they said the weekend would help them change their marriage?

Cautiously, she extended her fingers, beginning to bridge the gap between her and Carl.

Then a muffled sound of a harp played. Carl stepped away from her, lifting one finger up in the universal sign of "hold on a minute" as he pulled his phone from his pocket.

She swore to herself, her hand falling back down. Normally, she was the first to roll her eyes whenever anyone started in on how addicted everyone was to their devices, but now she saw their point. "Is that your office? Didn't you tell them not to call?"

Carl scowled at his phone. "That's weird. That's not my ringtone, and there's no cell service. Did you get the Wi-Fi password?"

"No, and I don't plan to. This is our weekend away, remember?"

"I've got to be reachable," he said, defensive. "My team is on a tight deadline right now, and they may need me."

"There's always a deadline."

"Don't start. You're just as bad."

He slipped his phone back into his pants pocket and returned to the fireplace, though he chose to stand farther away from her.

It might as well have been the Grand Canyon.

A soft knock came from the door.

Giving up on any attempt to regain the easy intimacy they had just enjoyed, Sylvia sighed. She turned from the fire.

"Don't answer it," Carl said as she stepped past him.

"They know we're here." She grabbed the room key from the bed where Carl had left it and opened the door.

Juliet stood on the other side. She had changed into a burgundy velvet gown and held a stack of familiar clothes in her arms. "Thanks for the… loan… they are super cute," she said in a tone more disappointed than apologetic.

Sylvia took the clothes, noting that Juliet's modern words were back. The girl was a mystery, among many in this place.

Juliet leaned in and whispered, "I have a gift for you. But *just* for you."

Before Sylvia could inquire further, Juliet turned and scurried down the hall, slipping back through the door to the great hall.

Keeping her back to the room and Carl, Sylvia lifted the folded scarf from the top of the pile.

Nestled among the folds of her blouse was another key. But unlike the heavy iron key to their room, this one looked as if it were spun from rose gold. Smaller and more delicate, the head of the key was crafted into a bouquet of flowers. Tied to it with a bit of twine was a folded square of parchment.

Sylvia opened the note and read the two words written in girlish script: *Use wisely.*

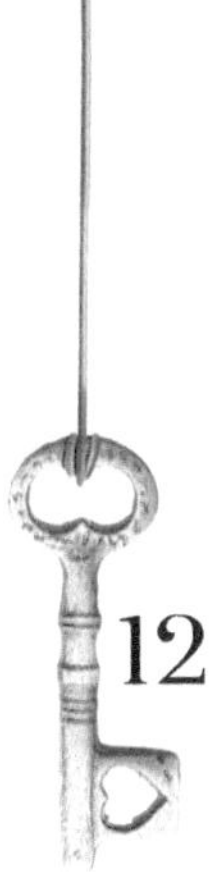

12

FROM WOE TO WONDER

"What did she want?"

She turned back to see Carl, sitting on the edge of the bed, scowling.

Sylvia glanced back down at the note.

Use wisely. Instead of a dot over the "I," the writer had drawn a heart.

Angie's final words floated in her memory: *Remember to use the key.* At the time, she thought Angie had meant the room key. But now, given Juliet's note…

Sylvia slipped both the key and note into her jeans pocket. She didn't want Carl to know about them. Not yet. He was already suspicious of Juliet. Better to let him cool down while she investigated on her own. She turned back to him, showing him the stack of clothes in her arms. "She just wanted to return my things."

"Good." Yawning, he dropped back down on the bed. "It feels like midnight."

Perfect. "Why don't you take a nap before dinner? I'll wake you."

"That sounds great, but are you sure it's okay for you?" He knew she never took naps.

She waved a hand. "Don't worry about me. I brought a book."

His eyes were already drooping. "You sure?"

"Positive."

Within moments, he had fallen asleep.

If only they could bottle Carl's ability to drop off, they could both quit the jobs they were shackled to.

Sylvia waited until his breathing deepened into snores, then quietly opened their door, and slipped out.

She half-expected Juliet to have returned, but the corridor was empty and deadly silent, except for the occasional crackle of the torches stuck into the iron wall sconces. Sylvia pulled the key from her pocket, wondering what it unlocked. Though it was much smaller than their room key, it still was big enough to open another door—maybe one of the two others in the corridor. She crept to the first door and tried to slip the key into the first lock, but it didn't fit.

On the second door, she was in luck. The key slipped in easily, and the door opened with a creak. She hesitated at the threshold, feeling butterflies in her stomach. She wasn't used to sneaking around, but she had to admit she felt more alive right now than she had in a while.

What had Angie said? The difference between excitement and nervousness was breath.

Sylvia drew in a deep breath, then entered the room. She took extra time to close the door to minimize any further creaking from its hinges.

The room was a private library. The five walls surrounding her created a hexagon, filled floor-to-ceiling with oversized books. In the center of the room was a large writing desk and chair. One of the books had been left open on the desk. An inkwell, quill, and still-lit candelabra were beside it.

The three candlesticks had barely burned down. Someone had been here recently.

Sylvia crossed to the desk. The oversized, leatherbound book lying open was very old. The pages were yellowed, and the words were handwritten in faded ink. She sat and had to lean forward to read:

Come, bitter death, I will not bargain with you. Here's to my love!

(Drinks.) The drugs work quickly, so with a kiss I die. (Dies.)

She recognized the story but confirmed it by gently closing the cover enough to read its title:

Romeo and Juliet.

The book was open to the scene where Romeo discovered Juliet in the tomb. Thinking she's gone, he killed himself. That one premature assumption had resulted in them both dead by suicide and forever apart.

But looking closer, Sylvia noticed a thin pink streak running through the second line of the passage, the stage action of Romeo drinking, saying his final line, then dying. A few words were added above the crossed-out segment:

Romeo sets aside the vial and shakes Juliet awake.

A small heart had been drawn over each "i," confirming the identity of the mystery editor.

"It took me hundreds of years and thousands of deaths to realize I could simply change it," a quiet voice said behind her.

Startled, Sylvia spun around. Standing just inside the door was Juliet.

She hadn't heard the girl come in, despite the door's hinges needing oiling.

The girl moved into the room with an easy grace. She joined Sylvia, peering at the page. "I had to cross out just twelve words. Such a small change, but it took me centuries to discover I could do it."

Sylvia looked up at the poised young woman beside her. The Valley Girl act had vanished and with it that sense of disingenuousness bothering

Sylvia from the moment they had met. But rather than the naive girl of the play, she felt as if she was standing before a mature woman.

"Who are you… *really?*"

The edges of Juliet's rosebud lips lifted, and her eyes twinkled. "You already know who *I* am, Mrs. McAllister. The more important question is who are you?"

"Me? You know who I am."

"Your name, but not who you are. Are you an author or merely a character? The one who creates the story or the one who is trapped by it?"

"What's that supposed to mean?" Sylvia asked but waved a hand in frustration. "Forget it. Never mind. I'm not interested in playing any more games. What's going on here? And don't answer my question with a question."

Impervious to Sylvia's brusqueness, Juliet smiled. "I play different roles, just like you. But I do it because it's fun. Because I refuse to be limited to the story assigned to me by the times, my culture, or my family. I am the author of my own story. Sometimes, that story is a romance, sometimes a comedy, often a mystery. I no longer need it to be a tragedy."

Juliet lifted the quill from its stand and dipped it into the inkwell. A single drop of magenta fell back into the well as she tapped the feather, then returned it to its stand.

"If this was a movie, my choice to play a silly, superficial girl would have more significance. Maybe I am a tragic figure compensating for a great loss. Or maybe I am a villain—a wolf in sheep's clothing—misleading my naive victims. Or maybe I am merely a secondary character whose only role is guiding the heroine in a quirky, yet important, way."

Sylvia rubbed her temples. She preferred the Valley Girl. This more cerebral version was giving her a headache.

"What I do and why I do it is not nearly as important as what *you* see and the story *you* make of it." Juliet lifted the heavy book from the desk and crossed to a bookcase. She tucked it back among the other volumes, then turned and leaned against the shelf. "As the lead of your own story, what do you think?"

"That I need an aspirin." Sylvia scrubbed her eyes with the balls of her hands, relieved she always kept some in her purse, but then she realized glumly it was back in their suite.

When she opened her eyes, the room was empty.

"Come on," she said aloud in frustration.

All she ever got in this place were more questions. She rose, feeling agitated and inexplicably ashamed. What did she have to feel bad about? And why did a girl of what—sixteen, seventeen—think she had the right to lecture her?

Angie's earlier words popped into her mind like champagne bubbles: *There are lessons, but no classes.*

This was ridiculous. She was alone, skulking around a library, instead of enjoying a relaxing weekend. Was she ever going to get a break?

Uninvited, Juliet's questions returned: *Are you the author or the character? The one who creates the story or the one who is trapped by it?*

"As if it were that easy," Sylvia said, then realized she was arguing with only herself. She blew out a breath. She had to get a grip, or she'd become as crazy as everybody else in this place.

Her eyes took in the hundreds of volumes surrounding her. Maybe she could order a cup of tea and get lost in a good book. Reading had always given her solace, even as a little girl.

Turning to the shelf nearest her, she ran her fingers along the spines as she read the titles: *Antony & Cleopatra, Elizabeth & Darcy, Helen & Menelaus, Catherine & Heathcliff.* The names of couples went on and on. She moved to another shelf: *Ross & Rachel, Carrie & Mr. Big, Mr. & Mrs. Claus.* The last made her smile. These books weren't just about famous couples from history or classical literature. Modern couples, even children's stories, were represented as well. Odd that the book titles were simply the couple's names and not the names of the stories or shows they were in.

Regardless, she could spend all afternoon diving into one or more of these books. *Ross & Rachel* would be the perfect distraction. She had binge-watched all ten seasons of *Friends* during the pandemic. Maybe their story was fanfiction. It would be fun to read about their relationship.

Her hand moved to the book but froze when she caught the title of the volume just to its left. The words were imprinted into the spine's dark leather, making them harder to read.

But as she stared now, there was no mistaking it:

Sylvia & Carl: A Tragedy in Five Acts.

THE PAPER TRAIL

hy did their story have a subtitle?

What did that matter? Sylvia chastised herself. The more relevant and disturbing point was the existence of a book—*a printed book*—with her and Carl's names. She reached out and swiped the shelf in front of it. Dust covered her fingertip.

It had been there a while.

A long while.

How could a book about them be here for the years it took to accumulate that much dust when they had only recently arrived?

The hair rose on her arms and the nape of her neck.

She wasn't going to kid herself and pretend the book was about another couple.

It was definitely theirs. She knew it as certainly as she now knew, against all logic and common sense, that Juliet wasn't merely a high schooler playing the famous heroine.

Both Juliet and this book were real.

Dizzy, she grabbed the shelf to steady herself. Her fingers touched the spine of her book, and a few pink sparkles leapt from the cover.

She yelped and jerked her hand away, stumbling back.

The sparks sizzled in midair like tiny fireworks, then winked out.

"Get hold of yourself," she said aloud, fighting every instinct to turn and run back to her room, back to Carl, back to the safety of reality.

But she didn't. Instead, she took one tentative step closer.

She had always hated when the main character of a movie or book, faced with something magical, denied it.

As a child, she longed to be Lucy in *The Lion, the Witch and the Wardrobe* and Alice in *Alice in Wonderland*. Girls lucky enough to find their way through portals into magical realms. Over time, she was forced to swap this longing for strength, self-reliance, and a practical, no-nonsense attitude, the cornerstones of her success. Magic played no part in her life.

Until now.

Before Sylvia could change her mind, she retrieved the volume from the shelf with shaking hands. No sparkles this time, but the leather felt warm and tingly to the touch.

She carried the book back to the desk. Her skin prickled with goosebumps, and she swallowed, her mouth dry.

Now that the moment was here, she suddenly understood why so many had run away from their chance… it was scarier than she would have imagined.

She sat and forced herself to open its cover. The familiar scent of old paper wafted from its pages. Moving the candelabra closer, she bent over to read the first page, chronicling the night in college when she first met Carl in the campus coffee shop.

Despite her nervousness, a corner of Sylvia's mouth lifted in satisfaction. Carl always insisted they met in chemistry class, but the proof she possessed the better memory—at least when it came to their relationship—was here in black and white. She couldn't wait to tell him.

Sylvia flipped the pages, feeling calmer as she read about their dates, their courtship, and their wedding. Before then, she was the first to scoff at the sentimentality of "your wedding should be the happiest day of your life," but in her case, it actually was. On the day they were married, she had experienced a new level of joy, as if an invisible cocoon of goodwill had surrounded and filled her and Carl. She hadn't expected that feeling—in fact, she had been reluctant to wed at all, having seen so many failed ones, especially her own parents'. That's how she knew the energy was real because it showed up unbidden, her best wedding gift. Though she never considered herself a religious woman, she had understood that day why many considered marriage a sacrament. The "wedding energy" had felt sacred. It was the only way she could adequately describe it, but of course, she would have felt foolish sharing her experience with anyone, even Carl.

Smiling, Sylvia continued to read and relive their first six months. The pages in the book only recounted highlights, but they reminded her how palpably she had felt that special energy during their first few months as newlyweds.

A dark thought interrupted her reminiscing: *If it was so strong, how could you have forgotten all about it?*

Her good mood faltered. At some point, that cocoon of effortless contentment had disappeared. But she had no idea when or why.

Impatient, she skimmed the rest of Act One, passing over the different moments of joy they had shared together.

When she read Act Two, she got her answer.

It wasn't a single, heartbreaking event. Or a terrible challenge or situation they faced. It wasn't like her favorite rom-coms or novels where the guy cheated or left his wife or disclosed an awful, irreparable secret.

No. It was much worse. The pages recounted her short-tempered-ness, his poor listening, her complaining to friends, his withdrawing, each of them taking sides, blaming each other, defending their positions…

As Sylvia continued to read, throat tightening, she realized she and Carl had punctured, torn, and eventually eradicated their cocoon of good-will through hundreds of insignificant reactions and unconscious choices.

From this vantage point, it was so clear they had made being right more important than being loving with one another.

Sylvia closed her eyes, feeling slightly sick to her stomach. She didn't want to read any more.

The subtitle was right. Their story was a tragedy.

They had taken a relationship, once offering all the love and caring and promise they could ever need, and treated it like garbage.

Each choice to react out of impatience or anger or indifference or hurt had been fleeting, but the residual effect was not. If she had only known what they would add up to, what damage and distance they would create, would she have been more conscious in each moment? Would she have made a better choice? Would Carl?

What does it matter now? What was done was done.

The weight of twenty-five years of mistakes made her shoulders ache, and she suddenly felt wearier than she could remember. How could they ever undo all those mistakes? They hadn't killed themselves, like the Romeo and Juliet of Shakespeare's original play, but they had surely killed their marriage.

She closed the cover of their story, feeling as if she were shutting the door on any possibility of a future together. But the truth, however painful to see, was quite literally in front of her in black and white.

It was time to finally face the facts: what they had created couldn't be undone.

Sylvia leaned forward and blew out two of the candles. The library fell into shadows, matching the gloom inside her. If there was no possibility of redemption, then the next steps were clear. She would return to their room and tell Carl it was over. It would be hard, but it was the only logical thing left to do. She suspected this was the one topic they wouldn't argue over.

She sighed, her breath fluttering the flame of the last remaining lit candle. She stared at it, giving herself one more moment before she took the hardest step of her life. As she watched, the tiny spark of light continued to battle the darkness around it.

A line from Juliet's story came to her unbidden:

But, soft, what light through yonder window breaks? It is the east, and Juliet is the sun.

Juliet might despise him, but Shakespeare had known a thing or two about light banishing the darkness.

Juliet is the sun.

The thought appeared, as small and powerful as the little flame.

Why not be like Juliet?

Sylvia jumped up and hurried to the shelf where Juliet had returned her play. Pulling it out, she cradled the oversized book in one arm and flipped the pages to the end.

There it was. The pink line that had saved her and Romeo's lives.

A narrow bridge to possibility.

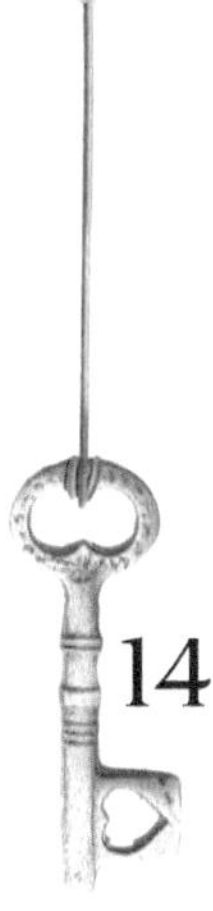

14

THE REVISION

Could it be that simple? Could she just scratch out her and Carl's mistakes? Could she rewrite their story?

"That's ridiculous," she said aloud. "There's no way."

Then what does it matter if you try? No one, except you, would ever know.

Sylvia reshelved Juliet's book and began pacing the room.

The problem was, unlike Juliet who had only one mistake to revise, she had literally hundreds of bad choices to change. Two decades' worth. Assuming her book worked in the same way as Juliet's did, she would have to write something new to correct each mistake. That would take days, maybe even weeks, of concentrated effort. And even if there was ample time, which there wasn't, how could she ensure she wouldn't make another, worse mistake in the rewrite?

The task was daunting. Glancing at her watch, she had about fifteen more minutes before Carl would wake up and come looking for her.

She didn't want him to find her scratching through a book in an attempt to rewrite their life. He would think it was crazy—and he'd be right.

She continued to pace back and forth across the short length of available space in the room, eyes never leaving the book, back open on the desk, taunting her.

Even if this did work—and she had only a single line in the play and Juliet's word as proof it would—how many of the necessary revisions could she make in just a few minutes? And which passages were the best ones to rewrite? Would it be better to change the problems at the beginning of their marriage, or try to fix what they were experiencing right now?

Would revising something years ago radically change their trajectory and present lives?

And what if some of those "mistakes" of their past needed to happen?

What if she deleted something essential to her or Carl? To their kids?

The last thought was the worst yet. How could she possibly take such a chance after all the blunders she had made?

The untampered pages waited. The chronicle of her many failures testified to her history of poor judgment.

No. She couldn't risk it. Even if that meant sacrificing her marriage, she would just have to live with the consequences of all her mistakes.

Sylvia shut the book and crossed the room to leave. But at the door, she paused, looking back one last time at the book, which waited on the desk.

But was not acting just as bad of a choice? Was denying this opportunity to turn around her relationship the worst choice of all?

She felt torn, lost. How could she know what was right and what was wrong?

Juliet made it appear so easy, even fun. Rather than drowning in a sea of choices, Juliet seemed to be surfing them. How did she do it?

Sylvia leaned on the door. The smooth, cool wood felt good against her back.

She knew now what resulted from reactivity and knee-jerk responses. Her story was filled with them.

She needed to do the opposite.

Taking in a deep breath, Sylvia fought against her sense of urgency and panic. She closed her eyes and willed herself to slow down.

I'm an intelligent, capable woman. There's got to be a way. If not, why would I have been given this opportunity? Please, whoever or whatever is behind all of this, let me see the clear path through.

Slowly exhaling, she opened her eyes, gazing again at the book cover, its title and subtitle stamped on the leather.

One thing was obvious. She no longer wanted to live a tragedy. She didn't deserve it nor did Carl. They were both good, caring people who somehow had gotten lost along the way.

She thought back to her conversation with Juliet. What had she said? That sometimes her story was a comedy, sometimes a mystery. But she no longer needed it to be a tragedy.

Sylvia & Carl: A Tragedy in Five Acts.

And suddenly, Sylvia knew exactly what to do.

Crossing back to the desk, she opened the book to the title page of the story.

She lifted the quill from its stand and tapped off the extra ink as she gathered her courage. With a trembling hand, she drew an unsteady line through the one word condemning her and Carl to problem after problem:

~~Tragedy~~

She stared at the word, surprised at how freeing simply crossing it out felt. Such a small act, but a big declaration to the universe—and an even bigger one to herself. Juliet was right. She had wasted too much time playing the tragic heroine, trapped in a story of her own making. Life was too short.

She paused. But what did she want instead?

Then, it came to her. Before she could overthink it, she wrote a single word replacement above the strike through:

Comedy

She grinned. Hadn't she wished on the drive that their marriage could be more like a rom-com? Thinking of it, she and Carl used to laugh together all the time. During the first few years of their marriage, he was always clowning around just to make her smile. Though he hadn't shown it in a while, he had a playful side. Remembering him that way made her feel good. It was one of the many reasons she had fallen in love with him.

And not just him. She had been a fun-loving person once. When she was a child, playing with her little brother, watching cartoons together, she'd enjoyed just being alive.

She wanted to reclaim that freedom. Not only for her marriage and husband, but for herself.

All of a sudden, she no longer felt discouraged. A small spark of hope had replaced it.

Sylvia felt sure that small spark was pink.

She bit her lip, a thrill running through her. Had it worked, and she was already feeling the change?

Before she could check further, a loud crash came from the outside hall.

Startled, Sylvia jumped back. The quill in her hand flung ink across the title page.

A wild braying grew louder, approaching the library door.

A moment later, an immense creature burst through.

Sylvia's mouth dropped open as it ran past her. Its antlers caught the edge of the table, jostling it. The ink pot toppled over onto the book. Magenta ink soaked the cover page like an open wound.

But Sylvia hadn't even noticed.

Because the only thing she could see was the six-foot beast that had skidded to a halt and was now panting in front of her. Unless her eyes were playing tricks on her, this creature with a glowing red nose was a reindeer.

A cartoon one.

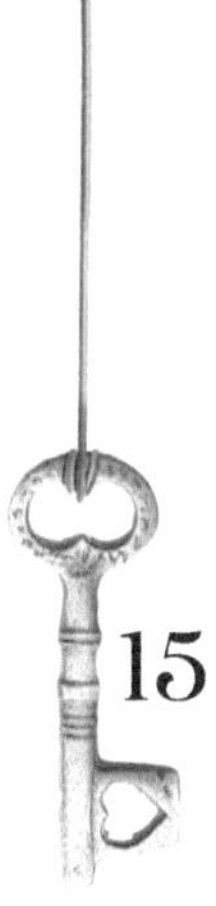

15

THE MR. & MRS. CLAUS ROOM

Sylvia stared openmouthed at the cartoon brought to technicolor life in front of her.

"Rudolph?" she whispered, recognizing the star of her favorite holiday cartoon. But it was impossible. He was an animation, a drawing on a celluloid sheet—how could he be here, panting in front of her, his red nose blinking on and off?

Then again how was this any less fantastic than what had already happened?

No, she thought, stunned. *This is definitely crazier.*

Rudolph snorted and pawed the ground impatiently. Each time, the desk and chair shook a little.

Sylvia noticed the fallen ink pot for the first time. Cursing, she righted it but had nothing to sop up the spilled ink. Her newly rewritten title page now looked like it should be in an Agatha Christie novel.

Not reassuring.

The door of the library was now open. Through it, another cartoon figure stepped into view, one tiny mitten-covered hand on her broad hips, the other carrying a large platter. She and the platter just managed to squeeze through. Her wide, red velvet skirts rustled from an untold number of petticoats underneath, and a matching crimson cap perched atop a snowy white mountain of curls. Her round face held an amused expression with bright blue eyes twinkling behind round-rimmed glasses.

Sylvia recognized Mrs. Claus immediately.

"Rudy! There you are, you naughty reindeer," she scolded. Her voice was high and musical with just a hint of accent that, rather strangely, sounded Canadian.

Rudolph dropped his head, the tip of his nose dimming. His big, baleful eyes stared up at her.

"Don't give me that look. Why did you run off just when your snack came out of the oven?"

His head still low, Rudolph eyed the platter dubiously.

"Come on, that's a good boy. Gobble up the healthy treat I've made for you while it's still warm," Mrs. Claus encouraged, holding out the enormous plate piled high with granola bars.

Sylvia squinted. Was that hay sticking out of them?

As if hearing her thoughts, Rudolph glanced toward the platter, then back to her, his upper lip curling.

"That bad, huh?" Sylvia asked.

Rudolph shuddered.

Ignoring the exchange, Mrs. Claus stepped further into the library, holding the platter high as she advanced on the reindeer.

Hurriedly, Rudolph retreated farther, his bulky frame backing up into the small room—right into Sylvia.

Reindeer rear end slammed against her. Sylvia lurched forward, falling into the beast.

As soon as she touched Rudolph's hindquarters, an electrical current shot through her hand. Her fingers shimmered, taking on an unnatural glow. Once the current raced up her hand and arm, the sleeve of her cashmere sweater turned from a muted beige to a puffed sleeve of red and white stripes.

Sylvia shrieked, pulling back her hand. But the intense tingling shot through her entire body. In dazed horror, she stared down at herself, now clothed in a red and white frilly dress trimmed with fake fur.

The matching fur-lined boots emerging from underneath the candy cane dress were cartoons.

Feeling faint, she swayed and reached out to the nearest chair to steady herself. The hand that grabbed the chair's back was drawn with thick, black outlines filled in with a bright band-aid color, nowhere close to a real flesh-tone. And not just her hand. Her arms. Her legs. Her entire body.

She was a cartoon.

And a hastily sketched one at that.

Mrs. Claus's face suddenly brightened when she caught sight of Sylvia. "Hello there! When did you appear?"

She carried the platter to the desk, setting it on top of the open book, and extended her hand.

But between her girth and the reindeer's, the expanse was too wide for her short arm. She tutted in exasperation, both hands returning to her hips.

"Rudy! This is exactly why you are not supposed to be in here. Now shoo. Or your name's going to the top of the naughty list."

The reindeer sniffed once at the platter of snacks, his nose glowing a sickly green, then beat a hasty retreat into the hall. Head low, he skulked at the doorway, imitating a more diminutive pet as best he could. Given that he looked to weigh well over a ton, he did an admirable job.

Path now free, Mrs. Claus approached Sylvia. "You must be Sylvia McAllister. We've been expecting you. I'm Mrs. Merriweather Claus, but please call me Merri."

Sylvia cautiously shook the other woman's hand, not knowing what to expect. But it felt the same as a normal handshake, firm and warm through the woolen mitten. How would Mrs. Claus's actual skin feel, given that it was drawn? Sylvia discreetly stroked the back of her own hand. It felt like her silicone phone cover.

She swallowed, her head dizzy with the tornado of questions whirling inside it.

Mrs. Claus watched her for a moment, then smiled sympathetically. "You look a bit perplexed, my dear. But don't worry. I'm happy to answer any questions."

Rudolph's excited braying came from the hall. As he peeked into the room from around the door, Mrs. Claus turned toward him. She picked up the platter and headed to meet him, shaking her head. "It makes no sense. He seems hungry, but for some reason won't touch the lovely snack I made especially for him."

Sylvia caught Rudolph rolling his eyes behind his mistress's back.

"I guess there's nothing for it but to give him an early dinner," she continued, squeezing back through the doorway. "After that, Sylvia, we can have a nice talk over a cup of hot tea. I'm sure you're parched after your long journey."

Sylvia hadn't noticed until then how dehydrated she was. She had left her water in the car, and the sip of Juliet's wine had only made her thirstier.

"That would be great. Thank you," she said, moving to join Mrs. Claus in the hall.

As soon as Sylvia stepped across the threshold, the medieval stone walls vanished, replaced by huge slabs of freshly baked gingerbread. At the top of the walls, where the crown molding would be, fanciful swirls of royal icing arced and swooped. A spicy-sweet aroma filled the room, making Sylvia's stomach growl.

Mrs. Claus giggled. "Sounds like a snack with that tea is in order."

But Sylvia hardly heard her. Besides an entrance at the far end of the corridor, there weren't any other doors like there had been in the castle. Fear gripped her as she realized that she was in a totally different place.

The castle and Carl were gone.

And her only way back was the library door.

Sylvia whirled around just in time to see Mrs. Claus reach past her to shut it with a click.

"Don't!" she exclaimed, pushing past Mrs. Claus to rattle the door handle, now a large chunk of rock candy. The exit was locked. She hurried to reach inside her pants pocket for the key, only to remember she no longer was wearing her jeans.

Her pants, pocket, and key were gone.

16

THE MISSING KEY

ylvia panicked. She dropped to the floor, hoping that maybe the key had fallen out. Her hands scrabbled on the soft gingerbread floor, but she already knew it was futile. If the key had slipped out of her pants, it would have been on a different floor in another world.

"It's alright. No need to upset yourself," Mrs. Claus's voice came from behind her, and a warm hand gently touched her shoulder. "Your husband's here."

Sylvia turned to look up at the cartoon woman. "Carl?"

"Yes, safe and sound."

Hand on her chest, Sylvia slumped against the wall. "Thank heavens. I'd thought I'd lost him."

Mrs. Claus smiled. "He's with Santa. Probably in the toyshop if I know my husband." Eyes twinkling, she looked at Sylvia. "But it's awfully sweet that you already miss him."

Before Sylvia could answer, Rudolph whined. His eyes were fixed on the closest wall sconce, fashioned from dark chocolate. Great streams of drool dripped from his mouth.

Mrs. Claus raised one mittened finger. "Don't even think about it."

Sylvia scrambled to her feet, sidestepping the growing pool dampening the pastry floor.

"Okay, boy. I'll get your dinner."

Nose brightened to a cherry red, Rudolph galloped down the hall.

Mrs. Claus followed him. "Best get to the kitchen and Rudolph's bowl. I'm not going to be able to hold him off much longer."

Sylvia trailed behind, processing everything around her. This world of gingerbread and icing was the same one from her favorite holiday cartoon as a child, brought to life. She and her brother, Tommy, would curl up with big mugs of hot cocoa to watch all the seasonal specials. The memory brought a smile to her lips. Somehow, feeling overly anxious in this warm, sweet-smelling place was impossible.

And another thought soothed her as well. Mrs. Claus showed no signs of shock at seeing her appear in the library. Therefore, this was not the first time other people had magically shown up.

As if reading her thoughts, her hostess said over her shoulder, "I'm glad I checked the library when I did. Couples usually show up in the morning. You've arrived rather late. Not to worry. Santa's already finished work for the day, so we have all the time we need."

Sylvia nodded, relieved to know she and Carl weren't in any immediate danger.

At the end of the corridor, two life-size nutcrackers flanked another doorway. They saluted Mrs. Claus as she walked between them into the kitchen.

Amazed to see another setting brought to life, Sylvia paused at the threshold. Here, Mrs. Claus would bake hundreds of treats for Santa and his elves. Like the hall, the room was warm and smelled of freshly baked cookies. It didn't take long to spot the source. Piles of sweets sat cooling across from a large oven, taking up an entire wall of the kitchen.

At first glance, it looked like a brick oven, but the bricks themselves were rectangles of shortbread.

How could a cookie oven bake without getting burned? Then again, why shouldn't it? This was a cartoon. Anything was possible.

A movement caught her attention: Rudolph edging toward the counter holding the piles. Star-shaped Linzer cookies dusted with powdered sugar, spicy-scented gingersnaps, and red velvet cookies with white chocolate chips were among dozens of different treats. The reindeer eyed them hungrily.

"They're not for you, Rudolph. At least not until after your dinner." Heading to a cupboard, Mrs. Claus pulled out a large box labeled "Reindeer Chow," carrying it to a bright red bowl in the corner. Mrs. Claus filled the massive bowl with the dried pet food.

Her back to him, Rudolph edged to the nearest counter and quietly snatched two Linzer cookies, swallowing them in one gulp and licking the powder sugar from his glowing nose before trotting over to his bowl.

"That's a good boy," Mrs. Claus cooed, petting his thick neck as he bent to eat. Sighing, she turned back to Sylvia. "It's a full-time job to combat the sweet-tooths in this place."

Sylvia glanced at the mounds of cookies. Then, why bake all of these?

Mrs. Claus followed her gaze and shrugged. "Hazards of the job. Go ahead and take a seat. I'll put on the kettle." She moved over to the red licorice stove next to the oven.

Sylvia crossed to a delicate table and chairs made from spun sugar. On it was a candy version of a Spode china set, featuring the classic Christmas tree design. Two green-rimmed cups and saucers waited. A marzipan poinsettia sat in the middle.

The spun-sugar chair was sturdier and heavier than its intricately drawn filigree first appeared. Sylvia was careful nonetheless, afraid to break off any bits. She perched on the edge while the kettle whistled a rendition of "Santa Claus is Coming to Town."

"I hope you like peppermint tea." Mrs. Claus carried a teapot and plate of cookies to the table. She filled each of their cups, then sat down with a soft grunt. "After a busy day, I love to put my feet up with a nice hot drink, don't you?"

"Thank you." Sylvia took a sip, curious to know if it would have any taste. In fact, it was the most delicious tea she had ever drunk. The shortbread was even better. Soft and buttery. As it melted in her mouth, a fond memory of her and Tommy tearing open their wrapped gifts on Christmas morning, their parents sitting together on the couch, filled her mind. One of the last times when they had enjoyed each other's company. "This is heavenly!"

"Close," Mrs. Claus agreed. "It's the Snow Queen's recipe. Her secret ingredient is nostalgia. It's the perfect sweetener with no extra calories. The tea is my own blend. Sugar-free. It helps me watch my waistline."

Given how much waistline there was to watch, Sylvia appreciated her efforts.

Mrs. Claus eyed the cookies hungrily, then took a quick sip of tea. "You must have many questions."

Nodding, Sylvia set down her cup. "A ton."

"Most of our visitors do."

"So, others, like Carl and me, have come here?"

"Oh yes! Many, many couples. Mr. Claus and I love entertaining."

"Do your guests…stay long?" Sylvia asked, trying her best to cover up her growing anxiety.

Mrs. Claus smiled reassuringly. "Don't worry. You're not trapped here. That's the first question our guests ask. I know our home here in the North Pole is quite different from where most come from."

"Quite different." Sylvia experienced a rush of relief. There was a way to get back. Thankfully, her hostess seemed willing to give her a straight answer. "So… please don't take this wrong, Mrs. Claus…"

"Merri, please," she reminded.

"Yes, Merri—your home is lovely—but…"

"How do you get back to yours?" Merri asked, finishing her sentence. "No offense taken at all. That's the second question everyone asks. And you already know the answer."

"I do?"

"Just find the key."

Sylvia frowned. "I tried looking for it. I think it's back in the library."

Merri giggled. "Not that key, dear. That was for the other room. The key from here."

Having finished his dinner, Rudolph snuck across the kitchen to snatch a gingersnap, then pranced over to Mrs. Claus. He circled around three times and dropped down at her feet. He was soon asleep, his snores joining the holiday music playing softly in the background.

"Another key from here…" Sylvia thought of Juliet, who had given her the library key. "Do you have it?"

The woman's eyes brightened. "That's a good question. In a sense yes… and no."

Inwardly, Sylvia cursed. Just when she thought she was going to get a straight answer.

Merri held up a hand. "Now wait. I can guide you, but only you can find yours because everyone's key is different." She stroked the reindeer's head, and he let out a contented sigh in his sleep. "This is mine."

"Rudolph?"

"He was the key to freeing myself from my miserable marriage."

17

ABOMINABLE HABITS

Sylvia had assumed she was looking for a room key. Something that would open a portal back to the world, but Merri was talking about something else entirely.

Leaning forward, the woman whispered conspiratorially, "I'm not sure you knew this, but Santa and I used to argue a lot."

Sylvia shook her head in surprise. Mr. and Mrs. Claus having marital trouble? Honestly, she never even considered their relationship. The two seemed so jolly. She had assumed all was well in the North Pole.

"You're not the first to be surprised." Merri accurately read Sylvia's expression. "It all seems so perfect here, doesn't it? But, in fact, it hasn't been easy."

"In what way?"

"Oh, many things, my dear. Imagine being married to one of the most beloved men in history. No one wants to hear my complaints. No one can ever believe that Santa does anything annoying."

Nodding, Sylvia took a sip of her tea. She could relate in her own way. Her friends adored Carl and were the first to defend him if she complained. Their appreciation should have lifted her mood, but it just made her lonelier.

"I bet that didn't help."

"I felt even more isolated up here. Santa had all his friends and his elves adored him. I couldn't go to any of them when I felt troubled, nor could I turn to my own family. They were overjoyed that I had snared the greatest guy in the world."

"It's hard when there isn't anyone who really understands. You end up feeling so lonely," Sylvia agreed.

Merri peered at her more closely. "Yes, that's it exactly."

"So, what did… *he* do?" Gossiping about Santa seemed almost sacrilegious. Sylvia could only imagine how difficult it was for Merri.

"Nothing terrible. I assure you. But he's partially human. He doesn't pick up after himself. He's a workaholic. He never takes time off. I was hoping for a honeymoon, but that never happened. The number of boys and girls increases every year, and toy production must keep up. It's a huge job for one senior citizen."

"But don't the elves help? It seems like—"

A deep growl interrupted her. Rudolph's usually bright red nose had darkened, matching his expression as he looked up at Merri.

Also noticing, she rose hurriedly. "But I don't want to get ahead of myself. Let me show you something." She set down her cup and left the room. Rudolph followed. Sylvia trailed behind, giving the reindeer a wide berth.

Merri led them into a large living room. A roaring fire blazed next to the biggest living Christmas tree Sylvia had ever seen. The tree grew up through an opening in the ceiling, where tiny snowflakes dusted its upper limbs. Hundreds of multicolored lights twinkled without the need for wire or plugs. She guessed the holidays lasted all year long in this version of the North Pole.

Sylvia recalled the room from the cartoon special, but in real life (if that's what she could call this), the living room had many more details. Thick cotton-candy carpets covered the floor. The walls may have been made of the same gingerbread as the hall and kitchen, but they were covered floor to ceiling with hundreds of holiday cards and children's drawings.

"All of my husband's clients." Expression softening, Merri gazed upon the walls. "He doesn't throw away any piece of mail from his boys and girls."

Sylvia's own refrigerator had been crowded back when Martin and Grace were little. She completely understood why Santa couldn't part with even one of the precious drawings. "That's very sweet."

"He is. He's the most generous man I've ever met."

Clearly, this woman loved her husband deeply. "Then, pardon me for asking, but why the problem?"

Merri turned back to Sylvia. "I would think you of all people would have the answer to that question."

Her response stung, but the compassion in Merri's eyes indicated insult hadn't been her intent. "You've been married for many years, yes?"

Reluctant to add anything, Sylvia only nodded.

"Two people, even two people in love, can get on each other's nerves."

"Sure."

Merri crossed to the fireplace, crowded with photos and hung stockings bulging with treats. "Love and judgment are bedfellows in most of us, but not very companionable ones."

Carl bugged Sylvia all the time. So how did Merri do it? From the little his wife had already shared, Santa wasn't the dream catch everyone assumed. How in the world could Merri live with his quirks without wanting to wring his neck? Cartoon or not, this woman had something Sylvia wanted.

Suddenly, she understood the kind of key she needed to find for herself.

Merri lifted a framed photo from the mantle and handed it to Sylvia. Set in a spun-sugar frame, the photo was of Mr. and Mrs. Claus. Next to them stood an enormous abominable snowman. Its white fur was matted and mangy, fangs bared in a snarl.

In a word, the creature was terrifying. Sylvia shuddered, hoping it wasn't somewhere around.

Merri took back the photo from Sylvia, gazing at it for a moment before gently replacing it on the mantle. "He's hideous, don't you think? But I like to keep that photo as a daily reminder."

"Of what?"

"That this creature once was Rudolph."

Hearing his name, Rudolph snorted. Despite his size, he was nothing like the horror in the picture.

"Come again. I didn't hear you correctly."

"You did. Abner showed up a year after Mr. Claus and I were married. Around the time we lost our newlywed glow."

"You named that *thing* Abner?" Sylvia asked.

Merri wrinkled her nose. "I was hoping a sweet name might sweeten its disposition. It didn't."

Suddenly, Merri's passing comment struck Sylvia. "What do you mean by 'newlywed glow?'"

She beamed. "It's hard to describe, but for the first year of our marriage it felt as if Mr. Claus and I were wrapped up in an invisible blanket, or better yet, that we shared a special light. That's why I call it a glow."

"Me too," Sylvia said. "I called it our wedding energy. I've never heard any other person talk about it."

"I don't think everyone experiences it. We're both fortunate."

"Yes, I suppose so." Sylvia recalled her own experience of energy, which had disappeared all too quickly. "Ours lasted for about six months."

Merri nodded sagely. "Strange how we could let something that precious fade away."

Offering Sylvia a seat on the sofa, Merri sat down in the love seat next to her.

The sponge-cake couch was more comfortable than the kitchen chair, but Sylvia was too intrigued to pay much attention. "What do you mean 'let it fade away?' It didn't disappear on its own?"

"About a year into our marriage, I started noticing the annoying things Santa did. He'd come home late without bothering to send word. He'd work on weekends, even though he'd promised we would spend time together. At breakfast, he refused anything healthy I cooked. He insisted on sugar cookies and milk while he lost himself in reviewing toy designs."

Sylvia thought of the meals she and Carl had shared, when neither of them had acknowledged each other, both so fixated on their cells. Ironically, their distance grew worse during the pandemic, even though they had spent 24/7 with each other.

"Santa would make a mess in the house and not clean up after himself. Lots of other tiny irritations popped up, and they just kept multiplying. I started resenting him for causing them."

"I get it. Believe me."

Merri's expression was filled with understanding. "This happens to most couples. In a way, it's the default mode. If we're not careful, it's easy to start taking our spouse for granted. It's as if our vision shifts. Rather than seeing all the wonderful qualities that we love in our spouse, we start seeing the behaviors and qualities we don't like."

Sylvia was floored. If only their couple's counselor had been so insightful. "How did you learn so much about relationships?"

Merri blushed. "Like I said, my friend Rudolph was the key. He showed up just after our first-year anniversary, looking like the thing you saw in the photo. At first, I tried to get rid of him. He certainly wasn't the dear he is today. Santa and I had a lot of scratches those first few weeks, let me tell you."

Sylvia thought of the wickedly sharp claws and fangs in the photo. "I can imagine."

"His favorite prank was to howl all night at the moon, and once, he even broke into the toyshop. It set us back months. He was especially fond of ripping the stuffing out of teddy bears."

"What happened? How did you turn it around?"

Merri shook her head. "It wasn't easy. We tried everything, but Abner made our life miserable, and we fell into even more arguments. I felt trapped—I couldn't see a way out."

Hearing about Merri's marriage struggles was a relief. "Everything you've said. It's as if you were talking about me. Abominable snowman aside," she quipped, trying to make light.

But Merri's eyes only held empathy. "It may feel like it at times, but you're not alone."

To her surprise, Sylvia's throat tightened, and her own eyes grew moist. She wasn't the emotional type normally. But instead of trying to cover it up or crack another joke, she simply nodded. Here was someone who knew what having a challenging relationship meant and had found a solution. Could the same approach work for her?

"One day I felt so wretched, I guess I was trying to find anything that might help cheer me up. I pulled out our wedding photos. As I flipped through them, I remembered our wedding day and how happy we were. As I was reminiscing, the most amazing thing happened. Abner began to change."

"What do you mean?"

"Not by much. He seemed a bit less fierce, his fur just a little less mangy. It took me several weeks before I realized that his appearance and disposition were tied to my thoughts."

Sylvia frowned. "I'm not sure I follow."

"It sounds more confusing than it is. Let me show you." Merri nudged the napping reindeer, who had joined them at the foot of the couch. He awoke with a snort. "Now, watch what happens."

Merri glanced over to a pair of muddy boots, long red hat, and belt thrown in a corner. She crossed the room, bending over to pick up the large hat and boots left there. Dirty prints stained the floor. Her face pinched with annoyance. She held up the discarded clothes. "Why does he leave his mess for me to tidy? I'm not his maid! Why can't he be more considerate? Does he think I just sit around the house all day with my feet up?"

Rudolph sat up, alert. As Merri continued to complain, his happy face contorted into a scowl matching his owner's. He rose onto his hind legs and lumbered over to her before falling back down onto all fours.

Merri's voice grew louder and more strident. "Couldn't he take two seconds to put away his things? And no matter how many times I ask him nicely to eat better, he never listens to me. The low-carb snacks I bake for him get thrown in the trash. It's infuriating."

Patches of white matted fur erupted on Rudolph's smooth back. His tiny hooves became claws. His red glowing nose disappeared as his face flattened and sprouted more mangy fur.

"Whoa!" Sylvia breathed.

Glaring at her, the half-reindeer, half-snowman growled. Sylvia shrank back against the couch.

Merri raised a hand as she retook her seat on the couch. "Okay, that's enough. Let's get you back, boy."

The creature snarled, mouth opening to reveal razor-sharp fangs as it advanced on them both. But Merri seemed unconcerned. "Santa may be untidy, but he's got a great heart, which is the important thing…"

The creature hesitated.

"And he's quick to laugh and loves having fun…"

The fur disappeared, revealing the reindeer's original smooth back.

The corners of Merri's mouth lifted. "After a long day of work, he wants to treat himself to snacks that he loves, and I can hardly blame him. I love them too. And I love the life we've created together. I love those moments when I catch him looking at me like he did when we were first dating."

All traces of the abominable snowman vanished. Rudolph's red nose glowed brightly again.

Sylvia released a breath she didn't know she had been holding. "That was amazing."

Merri bobbed her head at the compliment. "That's how Rudy helped me get rid of my habit of complaining."

What Sylvia had just witnessed was amazing, yes, but it didn't sit well with her. "But what you said about Santa's messiness. That was true, wasn't it? He should be more considerate. Why should you have to pick up after him?"

Mrs. Claus didn't respond.

Indignation rose up within her. Maybe Merri didn't realize the extent to which she was being taken advantage of. After all, she was drawn as a nineteenth-century housewife.

"Look, I admire how willing you are to look the other way, but it's not fair that you have to do that while he gets away with it. It's just not right."

A knowing smile lit Merri's face. "I'm so glad you brought up being right. Because that's it. That's it exactly."

Sylvia paused; a bit thrown by her hostess' response. "Uh, yeah. It should be right."

"Right!" Merri agreed enigmatically.

Sylvia threw up her hands. "Okay. What am I not getting?"

To her annoyance, Merri's grin widened. The woman was enjoying herself—and at Sylvia's expense. "You have a choice. Do you want to be right? Or loving?"

"Both," Sylvia answered immediately.

Merri held up a finger. "Sorry. You only get one."

"Why? I'm not going to dismiss what I know to be right to 'make nice' in my relationship."

Her outrage grew the more she thought of it. Without a sense of right and wrong, what would keep Carl, or anyone else for that matter, from doing anything they wanted? Where was the compass? How could she stand up for herself?

"Of course, you wouldn't," Merri agreed.

Sylvia's frown deepened. The woman's affability was maddening. Was she nothing more than a doormat? Willing to bend to anyone in front of her just to keep the peace? Clearly, her creators hadn't bothered to draw any boundaries because she had none. "I decided a long time ago, I'm not going to be anyone's doormat. Sorry, but I won't start now—and you shouldn't be either," Sylvia couldn't help but add. This conversation was absurd. Why was she even listening to a cartoon?

"That's very sweet of you to be concerned, but I'm certainly not that," Merri assured her.

"How could you not—"

"I'm not a doormat to others, but more importantly I'm not a doormat to my own reactions."

That stopped Sylvia short. "What do you mean?"

Mrs. Claus regarded her with compassion. "I know what I'm proposing seems ridiculous, coddling, even subservient to you. And I completely understand. All of that appears right from the perspective of the 'small self.'"

"I don't follow."

"The small self is those parts of us inside that feel threatened, insecure, scared, and hurt. The parts that feel they must be right and in control to stay safe."

Rudolph whined, nudging Merri, who patted his head. Nose blinking appreciatively, he leaned into her.

"Have you ever noticed that when you're feeling on top of the world things don't bother you as much?" Merri asked. "People's pettiness seems to be inconsequential when you're feeling good, but on other days, those same acts are really upsetting?"

"Sure. That happens when I'm driving in traffic. When I'm already stressed and someone cuts me off, I really lose it. But other times, when I feel good, I can get cut off, and it makes no difference."

Merri nodded. "That's exactly what I'm talking about. It's the same event, so what's the difference?"

"How I feel, of course, but what's that got to do with my marriage?"

"The need to be right comes from the small self, that same part that reacts when it judges something or someone as wrong."

Sylvia considered everything that Merri said. "So, you're saying I'm being a doormat to my small self?"

Before Merri could reply, there was a soft scratching at the front door.

"Why don't you answer it?"

Something about the simple request made Sylvia uneasy. The sound came again. A scratching so quiet it filled her with dread.

Mrs. Claus smiled kindly. "Go ahead, dear. It's for you."

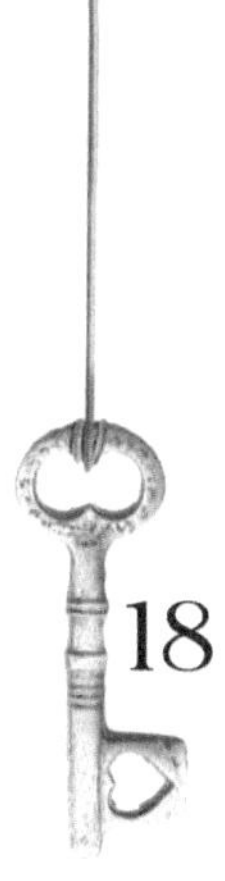

THE DOORMAT

Sylvia edged off the couch and slowly crossed the room. When she got to the front door, she glanced back at Merri, who nodded encouragingly.

Why did she feel so anxious? *Stop being ridiculous,* she scolded herself. *Anything making such a small sound can't be a real threat.*

But the tightness in her chest told her otherwise.

Grasping the handle, she took in a deep breath, then yanked the door open.

Huddled on the snowy doormat was a bedraggled baby bird, brown and gray feathers patchy amidst the down. It flapped its tiny wings weakly.

Sylvia's mouth fell open in shock. She knew this little bird.

But it couldn't be.

Blinking up at her with baleful eyes, the little bird let out a pitiful chirp.

"You can't…" she rasped.

"Someone you know?" Merri's gentle voice came from behind.

Sylvia couldn't answer, her throat suddenly too tight.

Its presence here—alive and in front of her—was impossible.

It died close to forty years ago.

The same day her parents split up. The last day of her childhood.

She was eight and her brother Tommy only five, playing in the backyard. Luckily for them, if they stayed at the far back fence, they couldn't hear their parents arguing. Their father's bellows… their mother's pleas.

That back corner was their oasis, their sanctuary.

That summer, Sylvia became convinced the backyard was magic, just like the wardrobe in one of her new favorite books, *The Lion, the Witch, and the Wardrobe.*

There was no other explanation for stumbling across the book, tucked away on the wrong shelf in the library. She was exactly like the girl who had discovered the magic wardrobe. She and Lucy were both eight. They were both alone. She was with her little brother, Tommy; Lucy was with her two brothers and sister. Both smart. Both torn away from their parents.

For different reasons, but it ended up the same.

It stood to reason that, like Lucy, she would discover a portal into another world. A world to help her mend her family, like Lucy had. And if the portal was anywhere, the fence dividing their backyard from the woods behind their house made the most sense. Her woods were even like those described in the book, except they weren't frozen.

She had spent a whole week searching the fence line, examining every inch of it for signs of a magic portal.

That's when she discovered the break in the back fence of their yard: three of the fence's slats slightly ajar, a secret door so small only she and her brother could wriggle through it. And, on the other side, a baby bird that had fallen from its nest. The tiny, defenseless creature would die without their help.

That *had* died, along with the hope that, if she wanted something badly enough, it would come true.

Blinking back tears, Sylvia forced herself to push away the memory as if stepping from a precipice.

But in front of her was no mere memory.

Somehow, that same baby bird had returned, staring up at her again, its tiny mouth open and hungry, its eyes pleading.

She suddenly felt as fragile and damaged as the broken eggshells surrounding the nestling. One more thing and she would crack.

"I'm sorry," she whispered. "I… I can't…"

She closed the front door and leaned against it, abruptly dizzy.

Behind her, Merri exhaled. A moment later, she flinched when the woman's warm hand touched her arm. "Are you okay?"

Sylvia pressed her eyes shut, fighting down the wave of emotions threatening to drown her.

"It's all right," Merri's voice soothed. "All in good time."

"I'd like to go home now," she said, her own voice sounding high and foreign to her.

After a few moments, the dizziness passed. When there was still no response, she opened her eyes.

Merri regarded her with such compassion that she felt totally exposed.

Sylvia turned from her and went back to the couch. Crossing her arms, she sat. "How do I get back home?"

Merri opened the front door. The baby bird was gone. The doormat was empty again. The only sign of what had been there was a small imprint in the snow.

Merri shut the door and returned to the couch, sitting next to Sylvia. "I'm afraid you need the key."

"Was that…?"

Merri nodded.

They both fell silent.

Despite the emotions still raging inside of her, Sylvia felt relief at facing a different kind of problem. One more like a puzzle than a tsunami. She was good at puzzles. They were made to be solved.

"There must be another key I can use. If there wasn't, then that… key…" She couldn't bring herself to name it. "…wouldn't have disappeared, would it? So, what do I do now? What have your previous guests done?"

She turned to Merri, who was chewing on a fingernail. Not a good sign.

"You must have seen this before. I can't have been the first."

No response.

"Have I?"

Merri pasted on a bright smile. "When it comes to love, there's always a way."

"Is there?" Sylvia thought back to her parents and the ugliness of their separation and ultimate divorce.

From her experience, when it came to love—*especially* love—there were rarely second chances.

SECOND (AND THIRD) CHANCES

They had searched every room of the Claus home in an attempt to find another key, but all they discovered were several stashes of stale cookies hidden by Rudolph, who had long since abandoned the hunt for an afternoon nap.

Sylvia sneezed.

"*Gesundheit*," squeaked a small elf beside her, who Merri had enlisted to help them. He pulled out a miniature handkerchief from his forest-green tunic and handed it to her. "I prefer the toyshop. It's a lot cleaner."

They both emerged from the hall closet, Sylvia dabbing at her nose. "No key in here," she called out.

"Nor here," Merri's muffled voice returned.

Frustrated and sweaty, Sylvia joined her hostess in a smaller room with a double bed. The shortbread headboard was decorated with royal icing and sprinkles. On either side were two stacks of gigantic macaroons functioning as nightstands.

Sylvia glanced around but couldn't see Merri anywhere. Then she caught sight of two tiny boots popping out from under the bed. A moment later, Merri wriggled out. Her white hair was dingy with dust.

"Jingle," Merri called, and the tiny elf hurried to her side. "Could you do a quick once-over? Especially under the bed?"

The elf made a big production of pulling out a gigantic pocket watch. It read 4:55 p.m.

"Is that the time already?" Mrs. Claus exclaimed.

"I can't stay late. The missus and I are going to see the little ones in *The Nutcracker*," the elf grumbled.

"Of course. You should be going. But, Jingle, would you mind awfully if you dusted in the morning?"

The elf harrumphed, mumbling to himself as he scurried from the room, "Six days, eight hours, and five minutes and I'm on vacation. And not one minute later."

So much for happy Santa's helpers, Sylvia thought, amused. Jingle sounded as burned-out as any of her office colleagues.

The dust motes from the elf's exit caught the remaining sunlight. Night would be upon them soon, and she wasn't eager to spend the evening on Mrs. Claus's couch, no matter how spongey. "What do we do now?"

Merri didn't answer immediately. She stared off into space, apparently deep in thought.

"Something Jingle just said has given me an idea."

"About *The Nutcracker*?"

"No. A holiday might just be what you need."

"A vacation? But isn't that what got me into this trouble in the first place?" If Carl hadn't fallen for the discounted price of the Magdalene, if he had just asked her first…but she stopped herself. If Merri had found another way to get home, she would take it, no matter what. "Nope. Never mind. Just tell me what I've got to do."

Eyes lighting up, Merri clapped excitedly. "Nicely done. That's the key that might work…give your judger a vacation."

"Come again?"

"It's a technique one of my more resistant guests found useful."

Sylvia couldn't argue with being lumped into that category, though it still rankled. "Just tell me how it works."

"Exactly what you just did. Each time you catch yourself moving into judgment, give the part of you who is judging a vacation," Merri said.

"That's it. That's the key." Sylvia couldn't hide her dubious reaction. "Then why didn't you…?" She stopped herself again. Nope. Her judgment was staying on vacation.

"I wish I had remembered it earlier." With a grimace, Merri guessed her thoughts. "Our afternoon would have been a lot less dusty."

Sylvia's hostess pulled an embroidered handkerchief from her apron pocket and delicately blew her nose. Maybe it was because she was a cartoon, but Merri had an uncanny ability to read her mind. Then again, maybe she was easier to read than she would like to admit.

"I suspect a bit of both," Merri answered.

Rudolph trotted into the bedroom and gave a sleepy snort.

"Okay, boy. I know. I know. But it's not quite dessert time yet." Merri gave him a scratch between his antlers, then turned back to Sylvia. "And, yes, there is a bit more to using this key. First, you must realize the part that is judging isn't the real you."

Sylvia raised an eyebrow. "Let me guess. The small self?"

"You remembered. I like to imagine it as that part of me who would rather be right than happy… or *loving*," she finished with emphasis.

"Back to that," Sylvia observed.

"Right again." Merri gigged at her own pun. "This part is so attached to being right, it will sacrifice everything, even its closest relationships, even its own happiness, to maintain the illusion."

"Are you saying it's not right?"

Merri studied her. "Which part of you wants to know?"

"What do you mean? It's me... I..." But then Sylvia paused because she realized who had asked the question. It was the part of her that wanted to be right—that *had* to be right. She never understood that part was different from herself. "I think I'm getting it."

Beaming, Merri gave her shoulder a pat. "I knew you were a fast learner."

"Right. It only took forty years," Sylvia muttered. It seemed so obvious now that she knew.

"Now, my dear, don't go and judge yourself," Mrs. Claus said. "Because then you're back doing the same thing with a different object. Whether you judge Carl or yourself, you're letting your judger take the lead..."

"Instead of letting it stay on vacation." Sylvia nodded a few times. "I see that, but how do you stop it when it's so... close?" She put a hand up to her nose.

Merri grinned. "It can be tricky at first, but, believe me, with a little practice, you'll know the difference. In fact, after a while, when you judge, it'll feel so obvious when your small self is temporarily back in control, you won't help but notice."

Sylvia shook her head, suddenly overwhelmed by all the layers. "This seems a lot bigger than a key. I feel like you're giving me a whole house to manage."

Merri laughed. "Speaking of, I feel like we both have a whole house full of dust on us. Let's wash up before dinner."

Sylvia let Merri guide her through a door adjacent to the bedroom.

Rudolph trotted behind them, the glow from his nose reflected in the large mirror that hung above the sink. Something about it caught her attention. Ignoring the other features of the bathroom, Sylvia tried to puzzle out what was bothering her.

And then it struck her.

The mirror was an actual mirror. It wasn't made of cookies, candy, or spun glass like every other feature of the Claus' home.

Why was it real? And more to the point, why did that fact fill her with dread?

"Merri!" a familiar voice called from outside, interrupting her thoughts.

Rudolph pawed the ground excitedly.

"In here, Santa," Mrs. Claus called, then turned back to Sylvia. "You and your husband should stay for dinner before you go."

The front door slammed shut. "I don't know what happened. One minute I was giving him a tour of my toyshop and the next minute he was gone." Santa Claus appeared at the door of the bathroom.

"Oh! Pardon me!" His rosy cheeks reddened in his wide-open, friendly face. He was exactly as Sylvia expected. Large, jolly, and sporting a red cap and coat, cinched with a huge black belt.

Merri gestured to them both. "Santa, this is Sylvia McAllister. Sylvia, this is my husband, Mr. Claus."

"Wow, it's an honor to meet you," Sylvia gushed. Here was the big man himself. She normally wasn't starstruck, but he was the stuff of children's dreams, her own included.

"Where's Carl, Santa?" Merri peered around her rotund husband.

Santa Claus shook his head, shrugging. "He just disappeared. Right when he was about to see how my toy train runs without a track." He glanced around the room. "He's not with you?"

His question was like cold water hitting her cheer. Where was her husband? Earlier, Merri had assured Carl was with Santa.

Merri shook her head. "We haven't seen him."

"Well, that's a bother," he grumbled. "I wanted to show him my collection of Christmas ornaments."

"Do your guests often disappear like that?" Sylvia didn't want to hear what she already suspected.

White brows furrowing, Santa absently pulled on his thick beard. "Can't say they do. Come to think of it, no one's vanished in that way… not in the middle of a tour."

"But no one else…" Merri began, then pursed her lips together.

"No one what?" Anxiety twisted her stomach. First, the baby bird disappearing, now Carl. Something was wrong. Something that, despite their many guests, Mrs. and Mr. Claus had never encountered. Were she and Carl that screwed up?

"No one what?" Sylvia pressed. "What's going on?"

Neither met her eyes. Santa scuffed the floor with his boot. Merri was suddenly preoccupied with wiping her hands on her apron.

"Please, if there's something I should know, you've got to tell me."

"Mrs. Claus, I don't think it's a good idea—" Santa began, but Merri stopped him with a gentle hand on his arm.

"She deserves to know."

"But isn't the point for them to get through this without…" He shrugged, lifting his black-gloved hands in surrender. "Alright, alright, my dear. You must do what you think is best, but I don't think they're going to like it."

"Who's they?" Sylvia looked from Santa to his wife, both of their expressions uncharacteristically grim. "Come on, don't leave me in the dark. I need your help—*we* need your help."

The couple exchanged worried looks. Rudolph whimpered and slunk out of the room.

After what felt to Sylvia like an eternity, Merri drew in a deep breath. "Have you ever heard of Narcissus?"

Sylvia nodded. Everyone knew the myth. It's where the term "narcissist" came from. "Someone who was so absorbed in his reflection…"

"That he disappeared… vanishing… forever." Merri's anxious eyes fixed on Sylvia, clearly trying to convey more than what she had said aloud.

But unfortunately, Sylvia didn't share her ability to read minds. "What does Narcissus have to do with Carl?"

Before Merri could continue, the sounds of muffled pounding stopped her.

Santa jumped. "Is that them?"

The three turned toward the sounds coming from the mirror above the sink.

Merri gasped.

"I told you they weren't going to like it," Santa said.

Carl's face filled the center of the mirror. His expression was desperate as his fists pounded the other side of the polished surface.

He was shouting, but what came through was hardly audible.

"Help!"

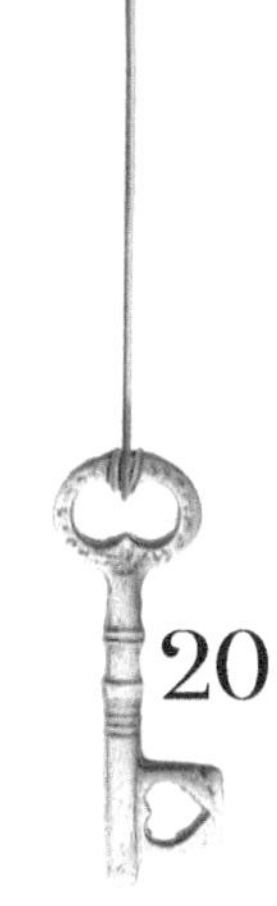

20

IF ALICE CAN...

"**C**arl!" Sylvia's hands moved of their own accord, darting forward, and reaching out to him.

As soon as her fingers touched it, the smooth surface rippled. Her husband's face disappeared, the glass surface transforming into a swirling maelstrom, sucking her in.

Before she knew what was happening, Sylvia was yanked off her feet. She tried bracing against the force, her free hand clawing at the sink's edge.

But her attempts were as futile as fighting a tornado.

Her skin, sinews, bones, tissue—her very essence—stretched and contracted, bending and reshaping as the whirlpool dragged her mercilessly into its cold black center.

Screaming, she tried to escape the force, but her limbs were no longer her own. She prayed she would black out before she was snapped in two.

Then just as suddenly, the pulling and the pain vanished, replaced by an utter stillness surrounding her. Calm, light and buoyant, like floating.

Relief and gratitude flooded her.

She had made it. She had survived.

Sylvia took in a deep breath… and gagged on the water she had just swallowed.

She coughed, and more water filled her mouth and throat.

She wasn't floating—

She was drowning!

Panic seized her, and she flailed wildly trying to escape.

When someone rapped sharply on her shoulder.

Instinctively, she turned, breaking the surface of the water.

Clean, life-restoring air hit her lungs, causing her to cough and gag up the water she had inhaled.

"Not the sharpest knife in the drawer," a voice said from somewhere above her.

"Don't be so mean," another voice said. "She almost drowned."

The first voice snorted. "Yeah, in about six inches of water."

Sylvia's coughing eventually subsided. She wiped the water from her eyes, noticing with relief that her hand was no longer a cartoon. She was back to herself again and out of the Claus home, but where? She blinked into the bright sunlight.

Once her eyes acclimated, she saw the water surrounding her wasn't the ocean or even a lake, but a shallow reflecting pool. Rising from the water next to her was a large marble pedestal. Still dazed and disoriented, she used it to pull herself to her knees. She panted there for a moment, dripping wet.

Her hands clutched the edges of a sundial set into the pedestal. The four matching arrows indicated 3, 6, 9 and 12 o'clock respectively. A thin rod at its center cast a shadow onto one of the quadrants. Sylvia studied the face of the sundial but found nothing to identify which hour was which. But given how bright the courtyard was, she guessed it might be near noon.

A soft rustling made her turn.

Standing on the side of the pool, looking down on her, was a beautiful, statuesque woman.

Sylvia shielded her eyes from the sun to get a better glance. No, not merely beautiful. As a southern Californian, she lived among some of the most attractive people in the world. Women and men whose exceptional beauty had lured them to Hollywood in hopes of making their mark and fortune.

But the woman towering regally above her made even those perfect people look like poor knockoffs against true haute couture. She was quite simply glorious.

The woman wore gold-beaded saffron robes cinched tightly at the waist accentuating her full breasts, only partially covered by a diaphanous amethyst shawl. Her hair was a thick chestnut, some pulled up in an intricately woven bun with plenty left to cascade down in curls. She wore no makeup that Sylvia could detect. She didn't need to. What could possibly enhance honey-colored skin or crystal blue eyes framed in thick, dark lashes? Her full mouth was an unbelievable deep rose that, under normal circumstances, would have been from lipstick or a permanent tint, but hers was natural. Around her long neck was a thick necklace of lapis lazuli, matching a coronet encircling her head.

But her most amazing feature was unseen. An invisible light emanated from her, an aura that Sylvia felt, rather than saw. It and she were magnetic.

The phrase that came to mind—the only one that even came close—was *Greek goddess*.

The woman nodded, whether in greeting or silent acknowledgement, Sylvia didn't know.

"Is she going to stay all day in that paddling pool?" a voice asked.

"Why can't you be nicer?" another voice whined.

Neither voice had come from the woman who continued to silently stare down at Sylvia. Her gaze was unwavering, but not confrontational. In fact, no emotion at all showed on her face.

Suddenly aware she was still in six inches of water, Sylvia scrambled out of the pool, awkward and self-conscious. She normally felt pretty good about her looks but compared to this woman… Sylvia wished the sun wasn't so bright. It revealed every one of her flaws. Who was she kidding? She would have to be in a pitch-black cave not to feel like a hag next to someone so outrageously gorgeous.

She took in a steadying breath, sweeping a hand over her tangled and dripping hair, and shaking off the excess water before extending it to the woman. "Hello, I'm Sylvia McAllister."

Perhaps the woman hadn't heard her because, without a word, she crossed to a nearby marble bench, languidly reclining as branches from the nearest citrus tree bent of their own accord to offer her shade.

Even the foliage couldn't help worshiping her.

Realizing she was staring open-mouthed, Sylvia turned away in haste and took in her surroundings. The reflecting pool ran the length of its center, with stone benches arranged along its sides. Perfuming the air was an abundance of blooming citrus trees, jasmine hedges, and rose bushes—all growing from ornate planters bordering the courtyard. Each planter was a balustrade of squat columns forming a decorative railing, accented every few feet with elaborate bronze finials. Behind them, giant versions of the same columns formed the peristyle's perimeter. There had been other voices—she had heard at least two—but, oddly, no one else was in the classic, interior courtyard.

"At this rate, we'll be here all day *and* night," the same strident voice complained.

Sylvia whipped her head in its direction but caught no one.

At least, no one standing. When she ventured a couple steps toward the voice, still muttering its complaints, she realized it wasn't coming from a person, but from one of the bronze planters decorating the courtyard.

She drew closer.

Not the planter, but one of its finials, which, under closer inspection, was a bronze mirror.

She bent to peer into the highly polished surface.

Glowering and grumbling was the face of a young woman she hadn't seen in years.

Her own.

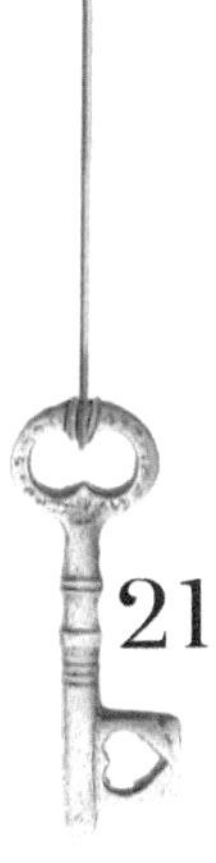

21

SPITTING IMAGE

"**W**hat are you staring at?" the face—*her face*—demanded. The younger self reflected in the bronze was in her late thirties. Her forehead was furrowed, her lips pursed. Her expression reminded Sylvia of how stressful that time had been, competing for her first executive position at the agency against a snake of a man. The type whose primary job was to get promoted, no matter who he destroyed in the process.

In contrast, her primary job was to do her actual job—thank you very much. How had there even been a competition? What choice was there between someone who consistently delivered successful marketing campaigns and someone who played golf and drank like a fish? Why couldn't the C-suite see that?

The face was still talking, but she was so caught up in her memories, she had missed it.

"Sorry, what?" Sylvia said.

"Earth to Sylvia!" the face jeered.

Sylvia's jaw clenched. She hated that phrase. Carl used to say that to her incessantly. Couldn't he see how hard she was trying? That, unlike him, she juggled three full-time jobs—her regular job, her new job playing the required political games to get the promotion, and her ongoing job of raising a 13- and 10-year-old, with all the defiance, anger, outbursts, and testing that came with their ages? Of course, she was distracted.

"You don't have to be sarcastic. Just repeat what you said."

The pinched face rolled her eyes dramatically.

Just like Carl. How many times had he criticized instead of helped? She didn't need much—a kind word, an encouragement, a gesture of support. Was that so hard?

Just like Carl.

Sylvia's panic returned in full force. "Carl. I forgot about Carl."

"Typical," the face remarked.

"Please. Just stop so I can hear myself think." Their bickering was incessant and she had no time to waste. Carl was in trouble… like these two, he was also in a mirror. She stepped forward. "Do you know how to reach Carl? Can you help me?"

The face smirked. "That's what I'm trying to do. Like I said, not the sharpest knife…"

"Give her a break. She's worried," another voice said.

Sylvia turned to the second voice, coming from a bronze mirror a few feet away. Her face again, but even younger, around her mid-twenties. This one wasn't pinched and disapproving like the first, but tight and anxious. At least someone appreciated how serious all of this was.

"I've no idea where Carl is, but do you? Can *you* help me?"

Eyes growing wide in alarm, the younger version of herself paled. "Me? What can I do? I'm maxed out already. Can't you see that? *You* should be helping *me.* I'm not asking for much… a kind word? An encouragement? A gesture of support? Is that so hard?"

This version was even more obnoxious than the first. She had never been that needy and self-absorbed… had she? Sylvia thought back to her mid-twenties when she was a young mother, overwhelmed with balancing her first baby's needs and a new career in marketing. At times, she had felt like a single mother, even though she and Carl were married—and from all outward appearances—happily so.

She had put up a good front, sharing the conventional gratitude her friends and family expected from a young mother with a "good man." But inside, she was a wreck. And the way everybody constantly congratulated her on her good fortune made her feel even more alone. The one person who should have gotten it, who was sharing the craziness of being a young parent with her, was as far away as everyone else: Carl.

Carl! Why did she keep forgetting about him?

Sylvia stared at the face in the second mirror, feeling its pull as if it were a current drawing her in. A dark thought dawned.

Was this what Merri meant about Narcissus?

With effort, she tore her gaze away from both mirrors and back across the courtyard to the woman still lounging on the bench…

Looking directly at her.

"What's going on?" Sylvia stormed around the reflecting pond to the woman, who no longer seemed nearly as enchanting. "And you can quit the silent treatment."

"Gladly," the woman replied.

Sylvia was momentarily taken aback, having expected more resistance. "Then why not say anything?"

The woman rose. "I did, but you didn't hear me. Not surprising. It's hard hearing another until you've heard yourself."

"No one ever listens to me!" the second mirror wailed from across the courtyard.

A snort came from the first mirror. "Yeah, no surprise there."

"You're so mean," the other voice whined. "Can't you see what I'm going through?"

Ignoring them, the woman gestured, taking in the courtyard. "Welcome to the Garden of Reflection. I am Helen."

Sylvia recalled the title of one of the books in Juliet's library: *Helen & Menelaus.* "You're Helen of Troy."

The woman inclined her head.

No wonder she had been so charmed earlier. If she recalled the legend correctly, Helen was the daughter of Zeus. A half-goddess, half-woman, venerated throughout the ancient world for her beauty.

Sylvia understood why. Had she been a man or held any predilection for other females, she too would have launched a thousand ships on this woman's behalf. But for some reason, she no longer felt quite as awestruck. It was a relief. It helped her to keep focused on the one thing that mattered—finding Carl.

"I'm searching for my husband, Carl McAllister. Is he here?"

"Here, there is all time and no time." Helen crossed to gaze down on the sundial. "Here the past is the present. The future is the past."

What was it about the women in these rooms? Were they contractually obligated to talk in riddles?

Mirroring her thoughts, the face in the first bronze blew out an exasperated breath. "Past, present, future—whatever! Who cares?!"

Helen regarded the bronze, then turned back to Sylvia. "You should care."

Her beautiful features turned grim as she glanced once again at the sundial.

"Because for you and your husband, time is running out."

# OBJECTS IN MIRROR ARE CLOSER THAN THEY APPEAR

Cold dread gripped Sylvia. "What do you mean?"

Following Helen's gaze to the sundial, Sylvia saw the rod's shadow had already moved from the first quadrant to the second. For an ordinary clock, that shift would take hours. But here, it had happened in just minutes. Her chest tightened. How much more time did she have? She couldn't be sure of anything in this place.

"He is in *The Between*." The shadow crossing Helen's face seemed to extend to the entire courtyard.

The bright and sunny place now was… murky… as if she were looking at it through a darkened mirror.

"The between?" Sylvia's own voice sounded odd and breathless.

"A place that waits between now and then, between here and there."

"Why is he there? What did he do?" But then Sylvia recalled Santa's nervousness, and the worry in Merri's face. Was this what Merri had been trying to warn her about? Was this 'between' place where Narcissus had vanished to forever?

A cold shiver ran up her spine, and she fought the urge to panic. No, that didn't make sense. Carl had been touring Santa's toyshop when he disappeared, not staring at himself. He hadn't made Narcissus's mistake… so what had caused him to disappear? As if in response, the image of shutting the door on the helpless baby bird flashed through her mind.

What if Carl hadn't done anything? What if this was all her fault? Guilt, old and familiar, rose within her, but she quickly willed it away, turning instead to Helen. "Why this happened doesn't matter. What matters is getting him out of there."

Helen shook her head. "If I knew where it was and how to get there, heaven knows I would have gone myself. I missed my chance a long, long time ago."

Something shifted in Helen. Her previous magnetism was replaced by a hauntedness and fragility. Whatever had happened to this woman was personal and deep. But unlike Juliet and Merri, Helen hadn't come through it victorious.

A chill ran through the courtyard, and Sylvia shivered.

What could defeat a goddess?

"I can't do this. I'm not strong enough. It's too much," her younger voice moaned.

Her younger self was right. How would she ever have a chance against a force that powerful? She had nothing to combat it. No idea what to do. No one to help her.

"Can't you shut up? Whine, whine, whine," the other voice said, its tone dripping with contempt. "You're pathetic!"

Sylvia's cheeks burned as if they had been slapped. No one talked to her like that. She readied herself to give the first mirror a piece of her mind when her earlier realization stopped her.

Narcissus's fatal flaw was getting caught up in his own reflection.

She looked at both images. The sarcastic one and the helpless one—they were opposites, except for one thing in common. Each time one of them talked, she felt a pull to believe them. To get lost in what they were saying. It was like being sucked into emotional quicksand. Her mood became theirs.

Not anymore.

Sylvia held up her hand. "That's enough from both of you."

The reflections fell silent, regarding her warily.

Sylvia closed her eyes, pushing away all the distractions to concentrate on the only important thing. Carl was trapped and needed her help. And if Helen was right, she had to come up with a way to free him—quickly.

To unlock a prison, you needed a key.

She thought of the keys Juliet and Merri gave her and hurried over to Helen. "If this is your room, you must have a key. Right? Why else would I be here?"

"Key?" Helen frowned.

"Each room has a key. What have you given the others who have visited you before?"

Helen shook her head. "There have been no others before you."

That stopped her short. "No one has visited you—ever?"

"You are the first," she said.

The idea had never occurred to her. Sylvia's heart sank. No wonder Helen didn't know about a key.

Did that mean she didn't have one?

Or worse yet—that she didn't need one because, unlike the other rooms, this place was a dead end?

A whimper came from the second mirror, but Sylvia ignored it. She wasn't going to give up, not without a fight. Not when Carl was in danger and needed her to find the way out. "We're both strong, capable women. Right?"

Helen smiled weakly. "Yes, we are that."

The courtyard brightened, just a bit. "Okay. Then we'll figure this out."

They both fell silent. Sylvia considered the problem. Maybe she wasn't as ill-equipped as she had first thought. She did have the experience of the two previous rooms as a guide. "Helen, what is it that you've learned while you've been here? Maybe we can find a key in that."

Helen considered a moment, then nodded once as if she had come to a decision. She crossed the courtyard, lowering herself to the bench next to the first mirror. As she did, the image inside the bronze shifted, dissolving from Sylvia's face to Helen's.

From her position on the bench, Helen couldn't see it, but clearly, she knew it was there. She placed a gentle hand on top of the bronze finial. "The one who was responsible for the war. The one who wouldn't stop until she got everything."

The crystal-blue eyes in the mirror had darkened to an aquamarine, seductive and magnetic. Knowing a bit about Helen's mythical standing, Sylvia wasn't surprised. Nevertheless, the reflection's gaze unsettled her deeply. Sylvia quickly averted her eyes.

"Can you imagine how *I* felt facing her for the first time? I turned away, just like you. I could not bear to look at her."

Scholars and playwrights had debated for centuries whether Helen was the cause of the Trojan war or simply a victim. Whether she had manipulated events or had been an innocent who was abducted and used by Paris. From what Sylvia saw, Helen was the former. The image in the mirror radiated duplicity. Given Helen's extraordinary beauty, she could have easily beguiled Paris, or anyone else for that matter.

Sylvia frowned. But the woman seated on the bench seemed incapable of such conniving.

Helen rose and moved to the next mirror, which changed as well. Sylvia's own image transformed into a younger version of Helen, her face streaked with tears, clearly afraid and desperate.

"The one who was taken, both in body and spirit," Helen said.

This was the version of Helen who had been abducted.

Sylvia glanced back and forth to the two diametrically opposed images in confusion. "Which one is true?"

"Both and neither." Helen continued around the perimeter of the central pool to the next mirror, which had been empty until then. As soon as she stepped in front of it, another image of Helen appeared. Unlike the first two, this face was twisted in grief.

Loss overwhelmed Sylvia, so deep she feared if she gazed upon that face for one more moment, she would be lost forever. She wrenched her eyes away from the image entrapped in the bronze.

"What happened to you?"

"I looked, but I didn't see… not in time. My blindness cost me my true love."

"Menelaus?" Sylvia recalled that the book in the library was named after them both, but she had seen no sign of him.

Helen nodded once. "We were reunited but never in our hearts. We acted the part of reconciled king and queen, but it was only a facsimile. A reflection of what we once had. Over time, our distance grew until one day I found myself here. A replica of our garden home, another facsimile, a reflection of a reflection."

"And your husband's not here with you?"

Helen shook her head.

The woman before her appeared so downtrodden that Sylvia hesitated to ask her anything more. But she had to, for Carl's sake. "Is he in *The Between*?"

"I do not know. He was there once as your husband is now. If I had been in possession of the key that you speak of, perhaps I might have been able to free him in time."

"But you must have it." Sylvia's panic returned. "Otherwise, I wouldn't be here. I have to believe that."

The compassion in Helen's expression brought tears to Sylvia's eyes.

"Please… I don't want to lose him." The words just tumbled out, but as soon as Sylvia uttered them, she realized they were true. Regardless of her and Carl's troubles, regardless of the fights and frustrations, she wanted him back. To rescue him, certainly, but also to be together. It was that simple. That was why she had stalled on separating, not due to weakness, or procrastination, or some other defect in her personality.

It was because she loved him.

Helen regarded her. "I believe you already have the key. And perhaps I can point you where to use it." She gestured toward the fourth mirror, still vacant.

Something inside her shrank back in fear, but Sylvia refused to indulge it. Not anymore. All her past complaining and questioning was a luxury she could no longer afford. "Tell me what I have to do. Whatever it takes."

"The hardest thing of all. Go back to the beginning."

23

THROUGH A GLASS DARKLY

Before the image formed, Sylvia knew what it would be.

What it had to be.

The thing she had been avoiding for decades, without even knowing it.

Feelings of shame rose within her, greeting the image swirling and resolving into herself at age eight, holding the lifeless baby bird in her hands.

Why did it have to be this? she thought bitterly.

All her life she had handled things. Taken care of everything and everyone. And this was her repayment? Being plagued by this one mistake she made so long ago?

The girl in the image was silent and tear-stained, the baby bird limp in her palms.

She had been watching over her little brother. At five, he didn't know any better than rushing into the woods to reach the little bird who had fallen from the nest.

As his older sister, it was her job to protect him, especially when her parents were arguing. That summer, her mom and dad didn't have time for anything else, not for fun, for games, for playing together.

All the things making those sticky, hot vacation days the best time of the year. She and her dad in the neighborhood pool, his laughter as he swung her high up into the air, only to let her go so she could plunge back into the cool water. Her mom tempting them to the side with homemade popsicles.

But that summer held no family outings or treats. Instead, angry, muffled voices echoed from behind closed doors. Then, as if the closed doors themselves were too much of a bother, the shouts erupted from any room at any time.

Closing the doors and pulling Tommy away became her job. No matter what they were doing, she would take him by the hand to some other place. Sometimes it was their bedroom. Sometimes it was at the far end of the backyard. She would hold him as he trembled, not saying a word, never saying a word, which made it all the worse.

She had to be the strong one, the alert one.

Just like Lucy.

As soon as she started Lucy's story, she knew a promise was hidden in its pages.

Magic was the way out, the way through.

It was waiting for her, but she had to find it.

And she knew just where to look.

Beyond the broken fence, there were woods filled with stillness and birdsong—a peaceful place where no angry voices were ever heard.

It was just like the woods Lucy had wandered into at the back of her wardrobe. She and Tommy hadn't met a talking fawn, but they did spot the baby bird.

Tommy had pointed first and rushed to get it, but Sylvia stopped him. They were already farther away from the fence than they had ever been, and she didn't know what else might be around.

"Stay here," she had ordered and ventured over to where the bird had fallen. It was chirping, the poor little thing. She looked high overhead into the large oak, spotting a nest in one of its top branches.

"Put it back." Tommy was suddenly next to her.

Startled, she yelled. "Tommy! You're not supposed to be here."

He stiffened, his eyes growing wide and filling with tears. Then he began to cry.

Sylvia felt awful for scaring him. She had never yelled at him before. Tommy's wails increased. She glanced back toward the fence, expecting one of her parents to show up any minute. If either caught them beyond the fence, she would get into trouble, not Tommy.

She had to calm him down. She reached out, patting him. "I'm sorry. I didn't mean to yell at you. Okay? I'll fix it."

Eyes imploring, he looked to her. "Promise."

"But only if you stop crying." She extended her finger. "Pinkie promise."

They shook. Then, satisfied, he wiped his eyes with his fists.

Keeping a hand on his shoulder, Sylvia considered the situation. The nest was far too high. She couldn't reach it.

But her dad could.

She squeezed Tommy's shoulder. "I've got an idea. Come on."

Very, very carefully, she gathered the little bird in her hands.

"Don't worry, little one. I've got you."

It didn't even struggle. It knew she was trying to help it.

Her dad always told her to care for those who were weaker. That's how she knew it was her job to take care of Tommy. And now the fallen chick. Her dad would be so happy and proud she rescued it.

She smiled to herself as she and Tommy stepped back through the fence and slowly made their way across the lawn to the back porch.

The tiny bird chirped up at her, then snuggled into her palms.

Amazed, she gazed down at it. She had seen enough animal shows to know most feared humans, especially little creatures in the wild.

This had to be a sign of the magic she had been waiting for—that her whole family had been waiting for.

So deep in her own thoughts, she didn't notice what was happening until Tommy gripped the side of her shirt.

"Open the door," she said.

When he didn't answer, she looked up from the bird to him.

He was pale, his eyes frightened, staring through the sliding glass door.

She followed his gaze. Her parents were arguing in the kitchen. But instead of simply yelling, her dad was shaking her mom. Her head jerked back and forth, and she was pleading with him.

Sylvia's baby brother whined next to her, but Sylvia couldn't take her eyes off her parents.

Suddenly, her dad stopped and stared down at her mom, as if noticing her for the first time. His eyes grew wide, and he stumbled away, letting go. Her mom fell back against the kitchen counter, then disappeared from sight.

Her dad lay against the counter, panting.

Normally, things were better when the shouting was over. But this quiet was different. Scarier. Like a rubber band stretched to the point of snapping.

Then, out of nowhere, her dad yelled like a trapped animal. He glanced around wildly, grabbing the first object within reach—a pot drying on the counter. Blindly, he turned and flung it. The pot flew across the kitchen in Sylvia's and Tommy's direction, smashing into the glass door directly overhead.

Sylvia shrieked and cringed, covering her head.

Tommy cried and ducked too.

Then all was silent.

Sylvia recovered first, looking through the now-splintered glass to her father, who stared back in horror.

Their eyes met. But she couldn't find her dad in the man who stared back at her in shock, in shame. This man was a stranger.

And that was far, far worse than their fight.

Sylvia couldn't watch this man for one more second. She turned from him, from all the awful ugliness beyond the cracked glass, and saw her little brother squatting at her feet.

Tommy. She had to protect him. Bending down to take his hand, she noticed what he was looking at.

She had dropped the baby bird. She had completely forgotten what she'd been holding.

The tiny bird was crumpled on the concrete of the back patio, head at a strange angle, tiny beak open but silent.

It was gone.

And with it, the magic.

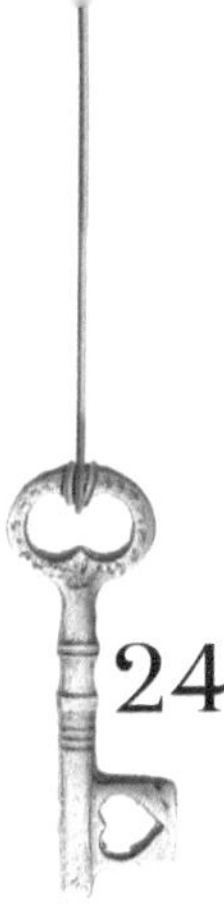

24

THE MIRROR CRACKED

At the same moment the pot hit the sliding glass door of her childhood home, the surface of the bronze mirror in front of her cracked. Startled, Sylvia stumbled back.

Her younger self stared out at her through a spiderweb of fissures.

Their eyes met, and a fresh wave of shame robbed Sylvia of breath, drowning her in all the condemnation and self-reproach she had avoided for decades. This was why she never looked back. It was too much. A moment longer and it would take her under forever. She gasped, fighting the impulse to run.

"Sylvia!" a familiar voice called from behind her.

She turned.

There, in the third mirror, was her husband.

"Carl!" she exclaimed and ran to him. She grasped the sides of the mirror, so relieved he was within her reach. "You're here! Are you okay?"

He scowled. "What do you think? What have you done to me, Sylvia?"

She stiffened, surprised and hurt by his reaction. But then, what did she expect? In her relief to see him, she had forgotten what he might have gone through. Of course, he was mad and had every right to be.

"I'm so sorry. But I'll get you out. I'll find a way," she promised with more confidence than she felt. Glancing over at the sundial, her breath caught. The shadow had already moved to the fourth and final quadrant. Hadn't it been in the second quadrant a few moments ago?

"I'm trapped in this place!" Carl's eyes darted around him, looking beyond what Sylvia could see in the mirror. "How could you have done this to me?"

"I didn't know." Guilt and panic rose within her. "No one told me what to do. But, Carl, let's not fight. We don't have time to waste. We have to work together to get you out."

"Easy for you to say," he spat, his face twisting in anger. "You're the one who should be in here, not me!"

"Don't you think I know that?" Hot tears stung her eyes. She wiped at them angrily.

"Sylvia," a woman's voice warned from far away, but she ignored it.

"What do you want me to say? That I feel terrible? Because I do."

Carl's face was a mask of bitterness. "How does that help me? You blew it, but I'm paying the price! I don't care how you feel."

Sylvia stumbled back from the mirror, her face as hot as if she'd been slapped. His venom stunned her. She understood why he'd be upset. It had been her fault. But she'd never seen Carl like this.

"Carl, stop—"

"I'm the one being punished for your blindness… your selfishness… your stupidity!"

"Don't talk to me like that!" Outrage flared in her, overcoming her remorse and fear.

"Why shouldn't I? That's what you are."

"What is wrong with you? I'm trying to help. Don't you get that? Can't you see…" But Sylvia stopped, realizing what was actually happening. What had been happening all along.

She wasn't arguing with Carl…

But with herself.

This was a mirror. She had never seen Carl like this because this wasn't Carl, just a reflection. And mirrors could only show one thing— what was in front of them.

This accusatory, angry Carl was merely a reflection of her—her attitude, her own condemnation.

She recalled Merri's warning.

The accusations had sounded familiar because they came from her, not from the *real* Carl. He couldn't begin to judge her in the ways she had judged herself. A litany of criticism so insidious and consistent that, over the years, it had become like street noise or elevator music, the background soundtrack of her life.

Sylvia glanced over to the eight-year-old girl, then back to the accusatory man. "Both are me," she said to herself. "Just like the other images in the mirror. They all reflect me."

"You have finally looked *and* seen," a gentle voice said.

Sylvia turned. Helen was rising from one of the benches. But rather than seeming pleased by her revelation, sadness filled Helen's face.

"You have now seen and yet…" Helen didn't finish.

The courtyard dimmed. Helen closed her eyes, but not before Sylvia caught them straying to the sundial with an expression of pain and defeat.

With dawning terror, Sylvia whirled back to the mirror.

Carl had vanished.

25

WORLDS APART

"Carl!" Sylvia shrieked, but the mirror only reflected her own stricken expression. She grasped the gold bronze edges, as if she could somehow span the chasm between them and pull him back to her.

Carl was gone.

Even though she knew the image in the mirror had been a reflection, cold fingers of fear still stole up her spine. Somehow, his image and the real Carl were connected. Now both were gone without a trace, without any way for her to find them. How could so much happen so quickly?

Sylvia glanced over at the sundial, stunned to see the shadow had moved past the fourth quadrant and back to the first. But only a moment had passed, hadn't it? How could she have possibly gotten him out with so little time?

"I am truly sorry," Helen said. The plants around her drooped as their mistress' shoulders sagged. Suddenly, she seemed old and tired, as if her own life energy had vanished with Carl.

The finality of her statement stole Sylvia's breath away. That was it? There were no more chances? Carl was gone... forever?

Part of her refused to believe it. But another part of her was all too familiar with finality. Life could change in an instant. Families could be torn apart by one choice… or the lack of it. Her life, Tommy's, and both her parents' lives had changed that one summer day.

Not even the day—just that one moment. The moment she and her father saw each other. The moment they both knew what had been seen could not be unseen, what had been witnessed couldn't be undone. That had been the turning point for them all.

Her father never met her eyes again. Just days later, he was packed up and gone. First, both parents assured Sylvia and Tommy his absence was only a "temporary" separation, but their empty promises fooled no one. Their divorce was quick and their estrangement final. Her father's visits occurred less and less, her mother's drinking more and more.

Age-old "if onlys" played on cue in her head. If only she had stayed away from that cursed glass door. If only she hadn't been so eager to gain her father's approval for saving the baby bird, which ended up dead anyway. If only…

Sylvia shook her head, willing away the memories and incessant second-guessing, and the shame and remorse that always accompanied them.

She didn't have to search back decades. The evidence was standing in front of her. This was what Helen had meant when she admitted her own blindness had cost her true love. Centuries ago, Helen had also run out of time and had been alone here ever since. Alone, except for her regrets, remorse, and loss.

Now Sylvia was alone. Without realizing it, she had run from this inevitability all her life, but it had finally caught up with her. No longer was it merely a fear hidden in the shadows. It was her reality now.

She would never see Carl again.

Sylvia thought back to just the day before, on their way to the Magdalene, and her irritation at not receiving the anniversary weekend she felt she deserved. As she did, that day-younger Sylvia appeared in the fourth mirror.

As she watched bitterly, the mirror-Sylvia glared at Carl and stewed in her own silent temper tantrum as petulantly as a child, staring out the car window, indulging herself once again with ideas of separation. She'd never imagined her ambivalence about the concept was based on a false assumption nothing would happen to her marriage without her choosing.

How could she have been so blind, given her own past? Of course, she could never have imagined the magic of the Magdalene, but lots of other circumstances outside of her control could have ended in their separation. Accidents. Disease. Fights that caused permanent damage. Life by its very nature was unpredictable, and yet she had arrogantly ignored what she knew to be true, assuming she would always be in control with plenty of time.

Every moment was precious. Why hadn't she remembered that anyone and anything could be taken away?

Why did she have to lose Carl to realize she didn't want to?

Sylvia turned away, sickened by herself. All the fight gone from her, she crossed back to Helen. "Why didn't you tell me? You could have stopped me from wasting so much time. If I had only known sooner every reflection was me…"

"If you had known sooner, what would that have changed?" Helen's voice was gentle and compassionate.

"I don't know… but it could have helped… it had to…" She faltered. Even to herself, her objections sounded hollow. Even if she had known who she was arguing with, nothing would have changed because nothing in *her* had changed. She had been arguing with herself for decades. Knowing a fact and realizing the truth were worlds apart.

As far apart as she and Carl were now.

"Realizing," Helen said, almost to herself. "Seeing with real eyes."

"But what good is that now? Carl's stuck who knows where, and I can't get to him."

A horrifying new thought came to her. Were they both trapped? Was she stuck here in this limbo, just as Carl was stuck in his? Was there no escape for either of them? With no way back to their family? Their lives?

Was she now truly and forever alone?

Sylvia's legs gave out from under her.

Helen caught hold of her, guiding her to a nearby bench. She settled next to Sylvia but said nothing to try and offer comfort. Helen of all people knew the heartbreak of this loss. The chasm of guilt and grief they had fallen into headfirst.

The courtyard dimmed further. Several blooms around them dropped their heads, shedding their petals, like tears, falling to the tiles underneath them.

They sat together in silence as the courtyard darkened to twilight.

At last, Helen spoke, "If it were in my power to act on your behalf, I would. I know too well how painful it is to be here, away from those you love."

A question came to Sylvia. "How long…" She hesitated, not sure she wanted the answer. "How long have you been here?"

The whole courtyard let out a low sigh.

"Millennia."

The reality was so horrible Sylvia's sense of fairness refused to accept it. "Just because you didn't realize something in time?" She shook her head. "No, that's not right. None of this seems right."

The Inn was supposed to be a place of reconciliation, not isolation. It was called the Magdalene, for heaven's sake! Named after the patron saint of prisoners. Sylvia thought back to her conversation with Angie and Harold, a lifetime ago. Wasn't the Inn there to support anyone who felt trapped? And she couldn't think of any four people more trapped than her, Helen, and their husbands.

"So why would the Inn put us through this? There must be more," Sylvia said aloud.

"Inn?"

"The Magdalene. This place is one of its rooms." Sylvia gestured to include the courtyard.

"It must be a place of great power to pull me here." Helen glanced around as if seeing her surroundings for the first time.

"Carl and I were even guaranteed that staying here would change the very nature of our relationship."

"Hasn't it?" Helen said with dark humor. Obligingly, the courtyard darkened further.

Sylvia ignored her and the growing gloom. "Not in the way we want—at least not in the way *I* want—and I'm 50 percent of this marriage."

Something awoke within her. Her grit. The one silver lining from that fateful summer day. It had never abandoned her. Like a trusted friend, it had always stayed by her side, especially during the tough times. And it was back now.

She stood, her dogged determination rising up with her. And with it, her confidence and reasoning returned as well.

"I don't buy any of this. It just doesn't make sense. If these mirrors are all reflections of me, then why is Carl trapped? What has any of this got to do with him?"

"I have often wondered that myself," Helen admitted, the twilight giving up the last of its color. "All this time and I have never found the answer."

Sylvia paced the courtyard, now obscured in shadow. It was aptly named. The Garden of Reflection. Like the mirrors, the courtyard itself followed its mistress's moods: bright and sunny when she was; dark and gloomy to reflect her discouragement and defeat. And Helen was clearly defeated.

The same question from earlier appeared again in her mind:

What could defeat a goddess?

But this time, the answer appeared. A response made even more profound because of its simplicity:

Herself.

The idea took form like a light in the darkness. Sylvia turned to Helen. "None of this had to do with Carl. *None* of it. And, heaven help me, I've been too blind to see that."

"Don't berate yourself. More than anyone, I know how useless it is." Helen gestured to the four mirrors. "It only feeds these creatures and keeps them, and us, in torment."

"Exactly," Sylvia said. "Because they're all just reflections of me… of what I say to myself, of all the ways I judge myself."

"That is the truth of the mirrors and of this garden." Helen's voice held a note of confusion. "But as you said, what does that matter? Knowing that doesn't free our husbands."

The clarity of their situation came to her in a rush, leaving her breathless. The pool. The mirrors. Their reflections. Carl's image, here, then gone again.

All of it, all of life, was merely a reflection.

"Helen, we never would have," Sylvia exclaimed, excitement growing within her. "Even if we had all the time in the world, we would *never* have freed our husbands."

"I don't understand." Helen frowned.

"It's not our husbands who are trapped—*only we are!*"

The goddess's eyes grew wide. "Can that be possible? But how can you know for sure?"

The entire courtyard began to glow with the soft light of an approaching dawn.

As everything became crystal clear, Sylvia laughed, joy and relief filling her.

"We're the ones who have been trapped, not them! And we also have the key!"

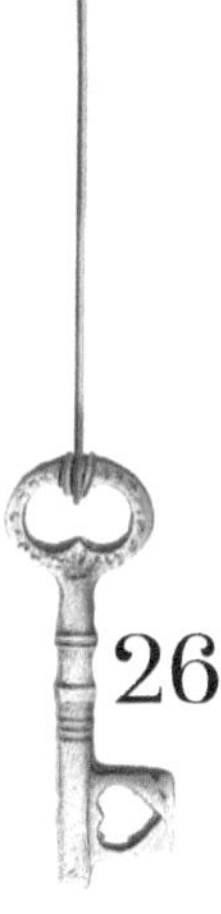

26

SELF-REFLECTION

The answer had been in front of her the entire time. From the moment she and Carl had stepped foot into the Magdalene—even before, when they were still out in the parking lot. Angie had given her the answer as she escorted them to the front doors:

That's the magic of it… both views are true… but it is a matter of choice.

Just for a moment, Sylvia had felt the weightiness of the statement, but as usual, so caught up in her own complaints and dissatisfaction, she dismissed the comment as unimportant. How wrong she had been.

Each room and every one of their hosts showed her the truth from a different vantage point. They had presented the different faces of the problem, allowing her to discover the one answer.

But like most revelations, it was obvious only after seeing it.

Sylvia exhaled, basking in the relief. There *was* a way out, a way through, back to her kids, her life, to Carl.

Excited, she hurried over to Helen, who was waiting for an explanation. "It's not enough just to know that these are our reflections. That's the first step, but simply knowing that fact doesn't solve anything."

"That much I understand. I've known the truth of the mirrors for centuries, and I'm still here. But how can you be sure we are the only ones who are trapped?"

"Because this is the Magdalene. It's about freedom. I'm certain of it. It's the reason why we're here. Recognizing that is the difference between us staying trapped and freeing ourselves." Sylvia looked around at the courtyard with fresh eyes. She saw it now as much as an opportunity as it was a trap. The way it functioned as both, depending on her perspective, was the point.

Wanting to hear more, Helen leaned forward. The light in the courtyard grew brighter.

Sylvia gestured to the four mirrors. Each now was filled with a younger part of herself. All silently waited, the bronze frames glinting in the sunlight. "These reflections aren't here just to torment us. They're here for a bigger purpose, just like everything in the Magdalene."

"What purpose is that?"

"They are here to be freed."

"Are you saying they are the ones that are trapped?"

Sylvia nodded. "And while they are, so are we."

Once she said it, it seemed so obvious. The Magdalene's magic didn't come in the way she had wished for as a child—wave a wand or discover a secret doorway and all her problems would vanish. That, in and of itself, would be another, subtler prison. She would always be dependent on outside forces for her own happiness.

Instead, the Magdalene offered the most powerful approach for true liberation. It provided opportunities—keys—to those who felt trapped so they could free themselves.

"If what you say is true, then the next question is obvious."

"How do we free them?" Sylvia said, reading someone else's mind for a change. "I believe the answer to that question is the real key of this garden."

As if in affirmation, that same intangible energy returned. The same energy Sylvia had first sensed radiated from Helen. But this time, it felt different, stronger, and purer, like the energy surrounding her and Carl when they first married. No doubt it, too, was a sign. A pointer she was heading in the right direction.

Helen sat up straighter, and the trees and flowers around her did as well. "It is my great fortune to have you as my honored guest, Sylvia McAllister. You are my rescuer."

Sylvia held up both hands. "Not me. I'm done with believing it's my job to rescue anyone. Only you can save yourself, Helen. I'm clear about that and just as confident that you can and will."

As Helen smiled, her face returned to its former radiance. "Rescuer, perhaps not, but teacher, most certainly."

Sylvia grinned, inclining her head at the compliment.

Helen arranged the layers of her mantle and dress to fall more gracefully across the bench, then looked back up. "I shall sit here, observe, and be an apt student."

Who would ever believe she, Sylvia McAllister, would be helping a real legend? But rather than feeling pressured, she was even more inspired to find the key to getting out. She felt more energized than she had in a long time. She thought of her former vivacious self in the hallway photo and realized—she was back.

Sylvia nodded once. "Let's do this!"

REUNION

ylvia crossed to the fourth mirror, where her youngest self waited. The poor thing cried silently, still holding onto the dead baby bird. This younger part of herself had been trapped in this terrible moment since it first happened decades ago. How could she free this child from her anguish? Compassion filled Sylvia, melting away any shame she had felt earlier. Why had she ever been so worried to face this scared little girl?

Sylvia squatted down, eye level to the child. As a mom, she knew what scared and upset children needed. Nothing fancy. Just caring and assurance they were not alone.

"Hi, honey," she said gently, treating this younger part as she would any upset child. "Is it okay if I stand next to you?"

The little girl looked up in surprise, as if she hadn't expected to be acknowledged. Still crying, she nodded once.

"I'm so sorry you had to go through all of this. I know how hard it was." Sylvia spoke the truth of her own experience.

Nodding, the girl began to sob harder. Her thin body shook as she cried.

"Oh, honey, I'm sorry. I'm so sorry about everything."

Through her sobs, the little girl managed to choke out, "It's… all my fault."

"No. Sweetheart, no. Believe me, it's not."

The eight-year-old shook her head fiercely, her braids swinging back and forth. "It's true. It's my fault. I'm the one who k-killed the bird…" she burst out, breaking into fresh sobs. "I made my dad go away."

Sylvia's heart ached for the little girl. The child's tears ran down her own cheeks. All this time she had blamed herself, totally convinced she was in the wrong. The bird dying… her father's leaving… her mother's drinking… her younger brother's struggles as a child, still plaguing him even as an adult. She had honestly believed it all started from her choices that one summer morning.

But now, seeing this innocent, little girl, it was clear that her belief was a terrible misunderstanding. It was a child's view of a complex situation. What a different view she held now.

Seeing through real eyes. The eyes of compassion and understanding.

"I want you to hear me. Can you do that?" Sylvia asked softly.

The girl looked up, her eyes streaming tears. After a moment, she nodded.

"You didn't do anything wrong. Do you hear that? You didn't do anything wrong," Sylvia repeated, gently but firmly. "What happened that day was not your fault."

"How do you know?" the child asked in a small voice, holding a tremulous note of defiance.

Inwardly, Sylvia smiled. The grit was already there, even as an eight-year-old.

"I know because I was there too."

The girl stared at her, eyes wide. "You were?"

She nodded. "I saw it all. That day and all the days after. And I want you to know what happened to your dad and mom and Tommy was not your fault either."

Sylvia thought back to how young both her kids were at eight, and what she had faced at the same age. A family torn apart. A father who left because he couldn't face his problems. A mother who collapsed into her own means of escape. Sylvia was left to raise her five-year-old brother. For Tommy's sake, she had become both mother and father. And despite everything, despite her own loss, she had become a lifeline of constancy and dependability.

She had done all of that while most kids her age were learning their multiplication tables and how to read books.

"You are amazing," Sylvia said in awe. "You are so courageous and loving."

"I am?" The little girl's already-high voice rose in surprise.

"You are. You are strong and caring… and I love you very much."

A weak, small smile touched the edges of the young girl's lips.

"I wish I could hold you right now. If I could, I would give you a big hug," Sylvia said.

The girl raised her arms. To Sylvia's amazement, the cracked face of the mirror melted away, and little Sylvia stepped forward into her embrace.

Sylvia pulled the child's tiny body in close. She closed her eyes and rocked her, stroking her hair, and telling her again and again how much she loved her.

As she did, more and more love filled her, warming her from the inside out. The child relaxed, and Sylvia realized how much she missed little arms around her neck, how much she had loved comforting her own two children when they were small. It was all they, and she, had ever needed to make the world right again.

As she continued to rock her younger self, the girl grew more and more insubstantial, but rather than concern, Sylvia felt as if a hole within her was being filled.

A part of her was finally coming home.

A moment later, she no longer felt this part of her as a little girl, but instead as a warm place of contentment and peace inside herself. Sylvia placed her hands over her heart, connecting with that warm place.

"Thank you for all that you've done."

Feeling complete, Sylvia opened her eyes. The mirror was vacant. The cracks were gone. The surface shone with new luster.

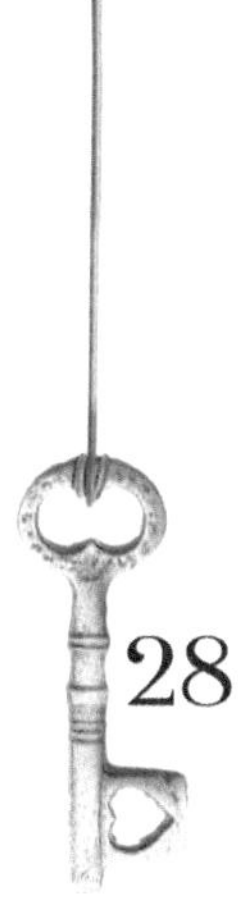

28

A CHANGE OF HEART

Sylvia rose and crossed to the next mirror, using the same key to free her twenty-year-old and herself.

Her younger self eyed her anxiously. "I can't do anything else," she argued, even though Sylvia hadn't said a word yet. "I'm overwhelmed as it is."

"I know you are. I can see that. I'm sorry no one else has."

The young mother blinked.

"And why wouldn't you be?" Sylvia continued. "Look at everything you're doing… and doing really well, I might add."

Her reflection's shoulders dropped. "Thanks for saying that." She drew in a long shaky breath. "It's just that, sometimes, I feel so alone."

"I get it and understand why you feel that way, but I want you to know that I'm with you," Sylvia assured her younger self. "You're never alone and we'll get through this together."

Gratitude and relief lit her expression as the reflection slowly disappeared.

Once again, the same feeling of being filled inside grew. How quickly and easily it was happening!

Was this all she ever needed? Just a little kindness and understanding?

She turned to the next mirror. The snarky Sylvia in her thirties rolled her eyes, but she wasn't fooled. She knew this one's game. Sarcasm was her protection, her shield against a myriad of hurts and disappointments. Like the other Sylvias, her thirty-year-old simply wanted to be heard.

She thought back to that time in her life and how hard she had struggled to raise her children and advance her career. That road had been a lonely one, and she had often wished someone—anyone—would have simply acknowledged her.

She knew now that someone was her. Sylvia gazed at her younger reflection. "You really are amazing."

The younger Sylvia snorted. "Only seeing that now, huh? About time."

Instead of reacting at the barb, Sylvia merely waited until the reflection met her eyes. It was easier now to see beyond the smokescreen of defense to a woman who cared deeply, who felt—and at times, hurt— deeply. Even easier to feel compassion and respect. "It took a little longer than I would have wanted, but, yeah, I see now."

"Promise me you won't turn into a total sap when I'm gone," the younger Sylvia said, as she began to fade.

"Gone?" Sylvia shook her head. "Nice try, but we're in this together. I need your sense of humor."

"True," the reflection said, a corner of her mouth lifting. "You'd be witless without me."

And then she was gone, Sylvia's self-judgment with her.

Sylvia stepped back from the mirror. Her heart felt both full and light at the same time.

She hadn't experienced this level of peace and freedom in years— perhaps ever.

Eager to face the fourth mirror and reclaim the final part of herself, Sylvia turned.

This reflection of her was only a day younger, the Sylvia who hadn't yet experienced the Magdalene.

Her reflection looked her up and down, apparently coming to an unfavorable conclusion. "Yes?" she asked, condescension mixed with impatience.

Inwardly, Sylvia winced. Had she always been so obnoxious and just not known it? No wonder Carl (and, alright, admittedly, many others) bristled when she approached.

Compassion, Sylvia, she reminded herself. Her acknowledgement of the other three reflections' struggles had been an immediate way to connect and a fast track to freedom for them and her both.

Putting on a sympathetic smile, she said, "I just wanted you to know I'm sorry you've been dealing with so much. I know how hard it is."

"Okay." The reflection glanced down at her Rolex. The message was unmistakable. Sylvia was wasting her time.

Perplexed, Sylvia regarded the reflection. Was this day-younger part of her so jaded even kindness couldn't reach her?

Her recent, renewed confidence dimmed. Maybe freedom from this place wouldn't be as easy as she thought.

The face in the mirror smiled tightly. "Are we done?"

"No, we're not done." Sylvia caught herself. She wasn't falling for that trap again. Battling herself just kept them both imprisoned.

Fine, she thought a bit resentfully. *If she needs a little extra time, so be it.*

Ironically, relating to and liberating much younger parts had been easier. Connecting with this part should have been the easiest because this reflection was the closest to who she really was. But maybe that was the very reason she was having difficulty staying open-hearted. Maybe they were too similar?

No, that didn't make sense either. Their similarity ended with their age. Because of her experiences at the Magdalene, she felt like an entirely different woman.

Over the last few hours, her view of herself, Carl, even the world, had changed so much. Recalling how she felt yesterday would be difficult, had the memory not been literally staring her in the face. She didn't want to be the cynical, suspicious, dissatisfied woman glaring back at her.

Life was too precious.

"I know what you're trying to do," the reflection in the mirror said. "I'm a marketing executive. I know all the tricks for persuading a prospect."

"You're not a prospect." Sylvia grimaced at the callous use of the marketing term. Potential customers were often called prospects, as if they were veins of gold just waiting to be mined. She shuddered. What seemed normal just a day ago was repugnant to her now.

Her reflection pointed at her. "You're trying to get me to act a certain way. To buy into what you're selling. Well, forget it. I'm not a simpleton. I'm not like those others who you can toss a few crumbs, a few 'caring' words, and they eat it up."

"Then what do you want?"

"I would think that was obvious. To be left alone in peace."

Sylvia considered this younger part, whose default was arrogant aloofness and dismissiveness. No matter how easy it was for her to react, she had to remember this reflection's ill-temper and shortness was merely a defense—and poor protection at that. No wonder she had felt tired all the time, with chronic neck and shoulder pain. She was walking around with a full suit of armor.

What could she do to pierce it?

No. That was the wrong question and approach. That was what she had done all her life. Fought for whatever she wanted. Played her life like a battlefield at the worst times, or a chessboard at the best, always planning out her moves in advance to win. That wasn't living. That was barely surviving.

"You're right," Sylvia said. "I was going through the motions, but to be perfectly honest, my heart wasn't in it. It was with the other younger parts of me. But with you, the compassion that had been real just a few minutes ago, changed from being a real response to a tactic to win you over."

That transformation had been so subtle. But hard to spot or not, it was the difference between something real and a really good imitation.

"Nicely done." The image licked her finger, marking one point on an invisible tally board. "A very elegant counter move."

Sylvia shook her head. "No moves and no more games. If I can't be authentic with you, then you're right. I don't deserve your trust."

The reflection raised her brows but said nothing.

"I wanted to wrap this all up in a tidy little bow so I could get out of here. But I get it now—that's just another level of self-deception. Because I'm not tidy. In fact, I'm a mess most of the time. When I'm honest with myself, most of my life is. I've stayed at my job for the paycheck and…" Sylvia faltered, hating to admit what had probably been obvious to everyone but herself. "And because it felt good to be the top dog. I told myself I was working for the good of the company and direct reports, but it was the prestige and control."

"I know. I was there."

"I don't even like the work. I don't think I ever did."

Sylvia closed her eyes, realizing she had avoided the real reasons she kept her job because they sounded so superficial and egotistical. But who was she fooling? Only herself. She was tired of all the pretense. It was time to accept herself fully, no matter if she deemed those parts as ugly or admirable. They were all her.

Sylvia considered other truths she had tried to hide from. "And if that wasn't bad enough, I'm hurt that my kids don't make me a priority." Embarrassed, she shook her head. "That sounds so pathetic."

"Not to me," her reflection said.

"I've done as much as I could to raise them as independent, healthy individuals. And now, I'm offended that they actually are. It's crazy but true."

Inside the mirror, the image shrugged. "Love is crazy."

"Don't I know it. I've wasted so much time finding fault with Carl, demanding he be perfect, when no one is perfect, least of all me." When she glanced up, her reflection watched her intently. "It's nice to have someone to talk to about this—and I'm not saying that just to flatter you."

Her reflection nodded. "I know. I can tell the difference."

"We both can." Then another thought occurred to her. "You know, it felt so good to finally face the memories I didn't even know I had been running from. It really was freeing… But I think I made an assumption when those other parts of me disappeared, and I felt better…"

Sylvia grappled to articulate something she was just beginning to be aware of. "It's as if when they disappeared, I thought those lonely, upset parts of me had gone. That they were somehow replaced… or maybe transformed… into happier parts of me."

"They weren't?"

Sylvia shrugged. "I don't know. I guess only time will tell. But here's what I'm trying to say. I was under the assumption *I* needed to be happy all the time now. That being in some state of perpetual happiness was the endgame." She held up her hand. "I'm not saying I don't want to be happy—"

"But as a goal, not a dictate," her reflection offered.

"Exactly. Because it sets up this whole other pressure, and then I'm back in the trap again."

"*We're* back in the trap again."

Then Sylvia suddenly got it. "That's why you're not going away, isn't it?"

The mirror-Sylvia smiled. Not a smirk, but a genuine smile.

In that moment, it was as if a window into herself had been cleaned, and she was able to see with crystal clarity. "People have called me a perfectionist all my life. But until now, I didn't realize what that was. *I* didn't just have to be perfect, my life had to be as well. Carl. Our marriage. My job. Everything. But that wasn't even the worst of it. The real trap was its flip side."

"Which is what?" her reflection asked.

"If something wasn't perfect, then I *couldn't* be happy. That's what I've been telling myself without ever knowing it. No wonder I was so dissatisfied! Nothing's ever going to be flawless. Not me. Not Carl. Nothing. It's not about trying to make everything perfect to be happy. It's about… just being happy. With myself. Accepting myself. Accepting it all. Loving it all."

Excitement bloomed in her as deeper and deeper levels of clarity appeared. It was as if they had been there, waiting for her the whole time.

"It's not even about loving it all *despite* the flaws—whether they're mine or anyone else's. That's just tolerance, which is only a subtler form of the same trap. It's about loving it all because there's beauty in being human—in the strengths as well as those precious parts inside who still need love.

"My other reflections were freed, not because I changed them, but because I accepted and loved them—loved me."

She put her hand over that warm place within, her own internal sun, and felt something long-lost returning—her wedding energy.

Catching a movement in her peripheral vision, she turned. Helen's face beamed with happiness, but this time, the energy wasn't coming from her. Helen nodded towards the final mirror.

Sylvia turned back. Her reflection glowed with that same energy.

Amazed, Sylvia looked down and saw the energy pouring out from her in rays of light. *This is the magic*, Sylvia realized in awe.

Her own heart was the secret door.

As the mirror shone brighter and brighter, the Sylvia within became more and more translucent.

Her face serene and radiant, she spoke.

"Welcome home."

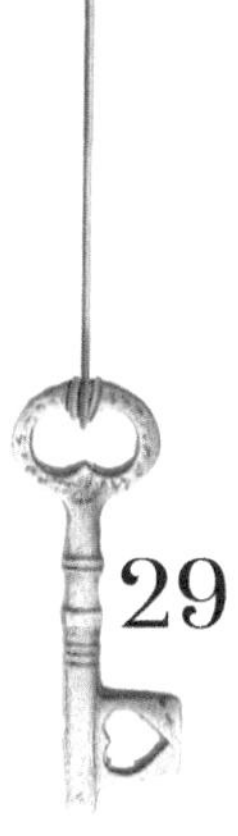

29

THE MASTER KEY

The next moment, Sylvia found herself back at the end of a familiar pink hallway.

A couple feet away, the door to the *Romeo & Juliet Room* flew open, and Carl charged out, stopping short just in time to skid to a halt before running into her.

"Carl," Sylvia exclaimed and threw her arms around him.

Her husband stiffened in surprise, then relaxed and wrapped his arms around her in a tight embrace.

"I've missed you so much," she said, her words muffled in his shoulder.

"I've missed you too."

And somehow, she knew both of them meant much more than their brief time apart at the Magdalene.

He was there, and she was finally, really with him.

Sylvia turned her face up to take him in, and he bent down, his lips meeting hers, soft and tender.

Surprisingly, she *wasn't* surprised at this rare and unguarded moment of true affection. It just seemed right. She simply relaxed into him, opening herself, as if it was the most natural thing in the world. Which it was.

As they kissed, she noticed that it didn't hold the passion from the beginning of their relationship.

It was better.

It held the attraction, the years together, the intimate knowledge of each other, and something more.

It held all of themselves—the devotion, the fights, the togetherness, the estrangement—everything.

And maybe because it held all those things, it felt deeper and truer.

At that moment, Sylvia realized she had found the most important key.

Everything, absolutely everything, was love.

Even while they denied its presence, love had always been there, an underground river, running throughout the years, without them knowing. A current of endless energy, connecting their hearts into one great heart, one eternal ocean of loving.

As Sylvia kissed her husband, that energy filled and surrounded them.

Tears streamed down her face, making their kisses salty.

Carl pulled back, his face open, his eyes filled as well. "You okay?"

She looked back, not bothering to wipe the tears from her cheeks, letting them be a benediction. "I am. You?"

"I am." He paused, then said, a sense of wonder in his voice, "More than okay. Fantastic, really."

"Yes, you are." She grinned.

He returned her smile. "I should take afternoon naps more often… and, just in case I haven't mentioned it lately, you're not so bad yourself, McAllister."

He hadn't used their nickname for one another in a long while. His eyes were bright and open. All traces of guardedness gone.

As if they were both seeing each other for the first time.

Expression turning tentative, he pulled back, as he searched her face in earnest. "Is this real? We both seem so different all of a sudden."

"It's real," she assured him.

"Wow," he breathed, considering a moment, then asked, "How are we going to hold onto this?"

She responded before she was even aware of the answer. "I'm not sure it's about holding onto it."

"But I don't want to lose this. It's… it's…" He searched for the word. "Magical."

"True magic." This was what she had yearned for even as a little girl. "I think it's less about gripping hold of it and more about letting go. Dealing with whatever comes but doing it together."

Carl paused, deep in thought. Then a quiet smile touched his lips. "I don't know why, but I keep recalling Gracie as a baby. Do you remember how long it took her to take her first steps?"

Sylvia smiled at the memory. "She would get so frustrated. You could tell she really wanted to walk, but she just couldn't figure out how… until she did."

He chuckled. "I think we're a bit like her."

"That's it exactly." Like their baby girl, they stumbled and fell again and again, learning how to stand up and walk together in love. It seemed silly now that they had ever judged each other.

"Let's not forget this moment," he said, then added wryly, "Guess we're not getting that free stay at the Taj Mahal."

Sylvia grinned. "Sorry about that, buddy. Guess our next vaca is on our dime."

"And I was so looking forward to the free naan."

They both laughed.

It was a miracle. Sharing a joke, enjoying being with each other, knowing that they both cherished this moment together more than a hundred Taj Mahals.

"I know we're booked here for a couple more days, but for some reason…" He shook his head. "I can't even say exactly why… but would you be too disappointed if we went home?"

We already are, she thought to herself but said, "Should we get our bags first?"

Carl clapped a hand on his forehead. "I totally forgot. I'm still foggy from all the bizarre dreams I had this afternoon. Weird, but so real. You won't believe it."

"Try me." Sylvia took his hand as they headed through the open door to *The Romeo & Juliet Room,* making sure it stayed wide open this time.

30

FINAL REVISIONS

The great hall was empty, though bright. All the candles were lit along the banquet tables.

"I'm sorry we won't be able to thank Juliet or Romeo," Sylvia said when they found the corridor leading to their room similarly empty.

Carl pulled out their room key from his pocket, and they moved across the pretty suite to collect their luggage.

Once again, Sylvia recalled how much had occurred since they both entered this room.

"I'd blame the wine for my wild dreams, but I didn't have any," Carl remarked.

"You sure they were dreams?" Sylvia stuffed her clothes back into her overnight bag.

Carl blew the air from his cheeks. "They better be, or your husband is having a nervous breakdown."

"There's a third option… This place could be magic."

"Oh, that's a definite," he said, taking her by surprise. "Just look at us."

Sylvia nodded. It didn't matter whether Carl believed in the literal or metaphorical magic of this place. What mattered was the true magic they shared.

When she didn't respond, Carl straightened up, giving her a curious glance. "How was your afternoon? What did you do while I had my nap?"

Was it only an afternoon? She could have sworn it was an entire lifetime.

"I went to the library—oh! That reminds me." She patted her pants, relieved to feel the library key back in her pocket. She snapped her luggage closed and grabbed her purse. "I have a quick stop before we go."

Carl followed, their luggage in hand.

Opening the door to the library, she stepped inside.

"This is cool." Carl set down their luggage. "Is this where you spent the afternoon?"

"Some of it." She crossed the room.

Their book was open on the desk just as she had left it, the cover page stained with magenta ink. But she moved to the bookshelf behind it in search of another's story.

The *Helen & Menelaus* volume was still where she had first seen it.

"What are you doing?"

"Checking on an old friend." Sylvia pulled the book from the shelf. Then, flipped the pages to the back, scanning the final paragraphs. What she saw filled her with joy.

Good for you, Helen.

She wasn't the only one who had found her happy ending.

"This book's a mess," Carl said.

Sylvia reshelved the book and turned to find her husband bent over the desk, his face mere inches from the cover page. He really could use new reading glasses.

She grimaced, crossing to him. "I had a run in with an inkwell and lost."

His forehead creased. Carl straightened. "This has our names on it."

"That's because it's our story."

"But it can't be. This book's an antique." He stopped, his expression growing more bewildered. "Syl, what's going on?"

Laughing, she patted his shoulder. "A lot. And nothing you need to worry about. I'll explain everything on the ride home."

Carl peered again at the book.

"The subtitle's scratched out, and the word 'comedy' is written above it—in your handwriting. Did you do that?"

Had it been the day before, his question would have set her off. She would have taken it as accusatory. And, if she were being totally honest, a tiny part of her would have *loved* nothing more than taking offense. But it really was just a tiny part... a tiny part still learning to love. The thought of Gracie as a baby made her smile. Yeah... she was okay with that.

"I did," she said, quietly triumphant that her response held no charge. She wasn't even pretending to be neutral. She actually was. That one small choice made her feel so empowered. "That was my attempt at trying to salvage things."

"What things?" Carl rubbed his brow. "I'm so lost."

"No problem." She kissed him on the cheek, and he put his arm around her. It truly was magic. Instead of his comment triggering a fight, they felt even closer. His question had inspired her. "You've given me a great idea!"

Immediately, he brightened. "I have? What?"

Sylvia picked up the quill and dipped it back into the ink. Bending over the cover page, she drew a line through her previous revision. Next to that, she wrote two words.

"A love story in five acts." Carl read the revised subtitle. "I like that, but can you keep up with me for five whole acts?" He waggled his eyebrows suggestively.

"Try me," she said, surprised to find she meant it.

Just as surprised, Carl gaped at her.

And, she had to admit, she was both delighted and a bit victorious at seeing his cheeks and ears turn pink.

Clearing his throat, he turned back to the book. "Now that I look at it again, there's something not quite…" He trailed off, turning his head back and forth in an admirable imitation of a cuckoo clock figurine.

She watched him, amused. "Not quite…?"

Eventually, Carl nodded to himself, apparently coming to his own conclusion, and held out his hand. "May I?"

"By all means." Intrigued, she gave him the quill.

He bent over the page and drew his own line through one of the words, writing in its substitute above.

When Sylvia read his words, her heart swelled. Any doubts she might have had about the magic staying with them were dispelled.

"A love story in endless acts," she said aloud.

They were going to be just fine.

31

ABOUT TIME

Carl locked the *Romeo & Juliet Room* and turned to her.

"Shall we?" He held out his arm.

She took his arm, enjoying the warmth of their bodies next to each other. Luggage in hand, they began the long walk through the labyrinth of halls to the lobby.

A mix of feelings filled her. Relief to be sure. They were together. And she was beyond grateful that everything had turned out better than she had dared to hope. The energy she once attributed to their wedding, which she now knew was simply their open hearts, was so present. She couldn't imagine how it could ever dissipate, let alone disappear.

But would a time come when they might slip back into their old habits of criticism, defensiveness, and separation? They felt so connected right now, it seemed hardly possible.

Even still, previous experience proved otherwise, and recalling how broken their marriage had been just the day before prompted its own set of questions.

Would that energy evaporate again as soon as they stepped out of the Magdalene and returned to their regular life? Would her heart close down as she reshouldered her responsibilities as a marketing executive? Could she even survive in a world where the love of power was prized over the power of love?

And what about Carl? Would he get so caught up in the never-ending litany of problems and projects he would forget what they had shared here? Would all they had fought so hard to regain be relegated to a treasured memory, put up on a shelf with other trinkets, where it would slowly fade from view?

She realized right then she couldn't go back to that. She didn't just feel different—she *was* different. An entirely new woman. She could never exist in the half-life she had tolerated before. Not now, when she had literally walked through the door into understanding who she truly was and what their relationship really meant.

Carl must have sensed her inner wrestling because he squeezed her arm. "I want to hear all about your afternoon. I know it's important."

Impulsively, she kissed him on the cheek.

He stopped, taking a step back and facing her with a mock glower. "Okay, that's it. What have you done with my wife?"

Sylvia laughed, slipping her arm back through his. "Returned her to you... after a long absence."

"Happy to have her back," he joked, then paused. His face growing serious, he pulled her into a tight hug.

The fierceness of her husband's embrace and the unexpected lump in her throat surprised her. Neither of them had shown any vulnerability in years.

It felt both awkward and wonderful.

When he finally spoke, his voice was low and thick with emotion. "I thought I had lost you... somewhere along the line... it's like you disappeared, and I didn't know what to do. How to find you."

She nodded against his shoulder. "I know."

"It wasn't only you. I was just as lost. I can feel that now that I'm back." He hugged her tighter. "I'm just happy we both are."

"Me too." She knew what he meant. Just being back together was a miracle by itself. But it was even bigger. They were both reclaiming themselves. For the first time, she felt whole.

Perfection really wasn't necessary. She simply needed to remember to reconnect with her heart.

And, even if she forgot that temporarily, she had keys to help her.

When Sylvia opened her eyes, her husband gazed back at her, his expression soft with love.

The two of them like this—whole within themselves as well as connected, filled, and surrounded by their love—*this* was what she had been looking for without ever realizing it.

This was true magic.

She only wished they could have more time, away from the pressures and problems of their regular life, in moments just like this. When everything was motionless and peaceful.

The pounding of running feet interrupted their moment of tranquility.

As Sylvia turned, a familiar figure tore around the corner and raced down the hallway to them.

"Thank goodness I found you!" Juliet all but collided into them.

"What are you doing here?" Sylvia asked in surprise. For some reason, she had assumed the couples couldn't leave their magic rooms.

Juliet bent over, holding up her hand as she caught her breath. Her blonde hair was tangled, and sweat stains appeared under the arms of her velvet gown. "We were… afraid you… had already left," she choked out between gasps.

"Just about to," Carl said. "But we're glad you caught us. Sylvia and I wanted to thank you for making our stay so memorable."

"Yeah, whatever," Juliet said and grabbed Sylvia's arm. "Come on."

Sylvia and Carl exchanged confused glances.

"Hello?" Juliet snapped her fingers. "I mean it. We've got to go." She pulled Sylvia down the hall, Carl following after.

Once they turned the corner, they heard the voices. The tomb-like silence of the Magdalene was gone. The din grew louder as they headed down the final hallway.

They stepped into the lobby and stared, stunned.

It was packed. Dozens of people milled around, shuffling from group to group.

Sylvia first thought it was a costume ball. The guests were dressed in outfits from different times and locations. Some women, like Juliet, wore medieval gowns, others hoop skirts, others a variety of indigenous clothing. The men's garments were as varied. One muscular, younger man was even in a loincloth.

But the atmosphere was decidedly non-celebratory. Some people wore dazed expressions. Many appeared fearful. A few of the women and men were crying.

"What's going on?" Sylvia turned to Juliet. "What's happened?"

Before Juliet could respond, Mrs. Claus hurried into the lobby.

Sylvia realized then who was crowding the lobby. Not guests, but the occupants of the Magdalene's rooms.

Mrs. Claus sped toward them, her cartoon feet making a rapid tapping sound.

Carl staggered back, his eyes growing wide as he dropped a few shades. "Is that... but that's impossible... she's a..."

Sylvia took his arm to steady him. "I was going to tell you later. Your dream wasn't one."

He fell silent, gaping like a beached fish.

"We're not supposed to be out here," Juliet whispered and jerked her chin toward the crowd. "Many of them didn't even know they were in rooms, let alone at the Magdalene. Romeo and I do—though he's too stubborn to admit it—because our room is often one of the first that guests are assigned to. But we've never, never, been out here with all these… creatures!"

Juliet stared at the cartoon standing next to her. Carl flinched, edging away from her.

Ignoring both Juliet and Carl's reaction, Merri looked around. "Mr. Claus and I knew our guests appeared from other places, but we never knew from where. We just followed the instructions."

"What instructions?" Sylvia asked, noticing that her new friend's usual demeanor had vanished. What had once been a perfectly drawn mountain of curls was now falling down. Long pieces of hair had escaped from Merri's updo. Her cap was askew, her glasses smudged, and her red woolen mittens were fraying.

"Notes that appeared on our mantel, telling us who to expect and what guidance might be helpful to share. They were always signed 'Angie & Harold.' But other than their signature, we didn't know anything about them. We just assumed they were the cartoonists. Who else could make the library door appear? Who else would leave us directions?"

"The tyranny of stage directions. I know it well," Juliet said darkly.

Merri eyed Juliet. "We were happy to follow them." She checked herself, flushing slightly. "Until today."

Merri smiled at Carl, who, still pale, managed to return it.

"That's how you knew about us," Sylvia said, pieces of the puzzle falling into place, "and how you got into the library."

"Yes, but your note was different, more detailed than usual. We never knew where couples like you went *after* us. Your note told of a room where none had arrived… nor left." Merri shuddered. "Certainly, every couple has their own unique path, but yours seemed even more so… and when Carl disappeared, it just confirmed that. I had never shared any of the cartoonist's directions before."

"Drawing outside the lines." Juliet nodded approvingly. "Nicely done, Mrs. C."

"I believe the phrase is coloring outside the lines," Carl said.

"Not on my rewrite, pal."

"We're both glad you made a different choice today," Sylvia said.

"Mr. Claus and I were so worried, but you proved yourself. You're here, free from that room, which means you passed the test and found the keys, even ones that were lost."

"Your help made all the difference." Sylvia wanted to reach out to her friend but forced herself not to. She didn't want a replay of what had happened the last time she had touched a cartoon. Instead, she glanced around the room at the groups of bewildered people. "But I still don't get why you all are out of your rooms."

"Angie and Harold must know," Carl said. "Have you asked them?"

Juliet's previous enthusiasm dimmed. "That's just it."

Expression suddenly grave, Merri added, "We can't."

"Angie and Harold are gone."

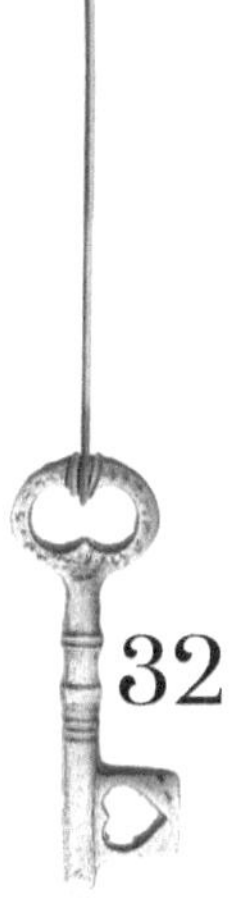

32

KEYS TO THE LAST RESORT

"They probably just stepped out. I'm sure they'll be back soon," Sylvia said.

The cartoon shook her head. "No, they won't. It's all in the note."

Sylvia and Carl followed Merri and Juliet through the crowd to the front desk.

Juliet handed the note to Sylvia. Not surprisingly, it was handwritten with pink ink. She read aloud:

Beloved Friends,

We regret that we can no longer be with you. We have been called back to headquarters...

"Headquarters?" Carl asked.

Juliet's eyes lifted heavenward.

"Oh! *The* Headquarters," Sylvia said. That answered a lot. No wonder the place was crammed with cupids. She continued reading:

And when the Boss calls, you answer.

"I guess you do," Carl muttered.

But never fear—we have left our beloved home in good hands. And just in time. We do ask that you all take good care of one another and this blessed place. Continue to support our guests in their liberation. Show them in your own special way that they are not only worthy of love—they are *love.*

Know you are always in our hearts.

Until we meet again,

Angie & Harold

Smiling at the two hearts drawn next to their signature, Sylvia returned the note to Juliet. "I'm sorry to see them leave."

"You and all of us," Juliet said, depressed. "They were the heart of this Inn."

"Come on. I don't believe that at all," Sylvia said offhandedly. But as soon as the words were out, a hush fell over the room, as if something had suddenly shifted in the energy of that moment. Everyone had felt it, and all eyes were on her now, heavy with anticipation. Sylvia felt it too. So, rather than filling the silence with a hasty response, she remained quiet, waiting herself.

Just a few hours ago, she couldn't have imagined this new reality. She and Carl were in the company of legends. Some were modern, many from ancient tales, but one truth united them: they were all teachers.

In that perfect lucid moment, Sylvia understood who she really stood before. These characters had willingly made the mistakes and borne their weight. They had stumbled, suffered setbacks, and persevered despite all the odds against them. And whether they had ultimately triumphed or failed, whether theirs was a happy or tragic ending, they had played their roles full out, again and again and again.

So that everyone—herself included—could learn and be inspired.

She stepped out from behind the front desk.

"You are the heart of this Inn," Sylvia said, addressing them, "and I'm certain Angie and Harold would agree with me. Each of you and the way you support not only guests, like Carl and I, but everyone, anywhere, who has read or seen or heard your stories. That's the heart and magic of this place. Without you, there would be no Magdalene."

She reached out to Carl, who took her hand, nodding his agreement. Behind him, she caught their reflection in the large mirror. They stood together, hands clasped, shoulders almost touching. Their easy intimacy reminded her of another pair. She and Carl were now *that* couple.

Ever practical, Carl added, "And don't worry. Angie and Harold's note says you're in good hands. We only just met them, but I'm confident they would never leave without finding great replacements."

"We *are* in good hands." Mrs. Claus glanced down at Sylvia's and Carl's, still clasped together.

Eyes agape, Carl followed her gaze down. "I didn't mean—"

"Of course!" Juliet exclaimed. "You two *are* the perfect replacements!"

And the crowd cheered their agreement.

Carl let go of Sylvia's hand to raise both of his. "Hold on, folks. Angie and Harold didn't ask us. They never said a word to us about any of this."

"They didn't need to," Merri said. "You proved you were capable by passing the test."

"What test?" Carl asked.

"The ultimate one."

"You chose love even when it seemed impossible," a voice said. "When even hope was lost."

Breath catching, Sylvia turned to the voice.

There, as radiant as ever, stood Helen. One of her arms was wrapped around a regal, gray-haired man wearing a brilliant azure robe and a crown of gold laurel leaves on his head.

"Helen!" Sylvia rushed toward her.

They hugged tightly. Once they had stepped apart, Helen gestured to the man standing beside her. "Sylvia, this is my husband, King Menelaus."

"I am honored to meet the one who has returned my love to me," the king said, bowing.

Sylvia's cheeks grew hot. It wasn't every day she got a compliment from a legendary king. "I can't tell you how glad I am to see you, your highness. And this is my husband, Carl."

Eyes dancing, Helen clasped Carl's hand. "It's a joy to meet you finally."

"Nice to meet you both," Carl said.

"You can't imagine how nice," Sylvia said, and both ladies laughed.

Bemused, Menelaus glanced from Sylvia to his wife, then back to Carl. "I sense we have much to learn from our wives."

"Don't we always," Carl agreed.

As Helen and Menelaus greeted the others, what Merri had said struck Sylvia. "Was Helen's room the test? Do you suppose that's why no one had been there before?" she asked Merri, but Juliet answered first.

"I suppose each guest is tested. Each must find the keys most helpful for them and make the ultimate choice."

"But you?" Merri glanced fondly at Helen and Menelaus, then back to Sylvia. "Your opportunity was unique. Perhaps because the Inn was looking for new management. Why else would you be here at this time? Your decision to choose love above all else not only served yourselves; it has served others."

"For which we are both eternally grateful." Helen gazed up at her husband, who kissed her tenderly on the cheek.

"That is how we all know," Juliet gestured to the entire crowd standing around them, "that you two will carry on the legacy of love that is the Magdalene."

"That's kind of you," Carl said to the group, "but it's impossible. We can't be Angie and Harold's replacements."

"Can't we?" Sylvia glanced back up to their reflection in the mirror. She had been more right than she had even known. Now, they could really be *that* couple.

Carl turned to her. "Are you kidding? Sylvia, we can't stay here."

"Why not?" she said, warming to the idea. It was crazy, yes, but what Merri said made sense. And hadn't she just wished for a respite? A time out from all the pressures and problems of their lives so she and Carl had the freedom to get to know each other again? To let their hearts take the lead and all the keys they had learned sink in? "Why can't we stay?"

"Because we have jobs. Because we have responsibilities," Carl said.

"Jobs neither of us can stand. Responsibilities that suck all the joy and life out of us and our relationship." She faced him, taking both his hands in hers. "Honey, think about it for a minute. Wouldn't it be nice to start fresh? Even if it were just for a while?"

"Just a while?"

"Sure, we could try it out as an experiment. We could take an extended vacation. Heaven knows, neither of us has taken much time off. I know I've accumulated weeks and weeks of it." The more she talked about it, the more enthused she felt.

"I have over three months."

"What if we did something crazy for once? Something totally out of the box. What if we chose us?" She placed her hand on his cheek, knowing what an outrageous act it would be for her practical husband. But in only a moment, a tiny spark of hope appeared amidst his bewilderment and skepticism, like daybreak. That small spark spread across his face, lighting it up, reaching his eyes, which filled with excitement.

"Why not?" he said. "Why not choose us?"

The crowd cheered again and surged forward, dozens of men and women coming to shake their hands and pat them on the back.

Sylvia's face began to ache, she was grinning so much. She felt freer than she had in years, perhaps freer than ever in her life. And from the lightness of his expression, Carl felt the same. Sure, there would be a lot of decisions to make, a lot to clarify, and even more to learn.

But she knew, in time, it would all work itself out.

Amid all the well wishes, Romeo approached with a leather satchel. He handed it to Carl, who sagged under its weight.

"What's in this?" Carl set the bag down with a thud.

"The keys to the Magdalene. They're yours now. One to each room."

Sylvia squatted to open the bag. Inside were dozens, if not hundreds, of keys. All of different shapes and sizes. "Wow," she breathed.

At the top of the pile, one key glowed a blush rose. She pulled it out from the bag and showed it to Carl.

"Why is it glowing?" he asked.

"It means that it will be needed," Juliet said. "The Magdalene always chooses the room right before the guests arrive."

Somewhere, a lute began to play. Menelaus took that as his cue to escort his queen to the middle of the lobby and began a courtly dance. Several other couples joined them, some of which Sylvia recognized: Scarlett and Rhett, Darcy and Elizabeth, Antony and Cleopatra.

All too soon, they would need to prepare for the upcoming guest. Everyone would have to return to their own rooms, and there was surely plenty else to do.

But for now, for this one blessed moment, simply watching the dance was glorious. Every dancer chose different steps. None better or worse. Each dancer and each step celebrated freedom and love: the true heart of the Magdalene.

She felt a gentle nudge at her shoulder.

She turned to Carl, who nodded at the dancers. "It's been a long time."

For a lot of things, she mused. For the first time in a long time, she was excited about the possibilities.

"May I?" Carl offered his hand.

"Always." Sylvia gave him her own.

And they too began to dance.

EPILOGUE
SEVEN MINUTES LATER...

An earsplitting alarm cut through the lobby, shattering the serenity of the scene.

Someone screamed.

Abruptly, the dancers halted, bumping into each other.

Scarlett O'Hara stopped, but her heavy hooped skirt kept going, swinging wide and knocking into Sylvia, who fell against Carl.

"What in the world?" Carl blurted out as he collided into Cleopatra, earning him a dark glare from Antony.

"What's wrong?" Sylvia shouted over the din. "Is there a fire?"

"The next guests. They've arrived early," Juliet yelled back, hurrying to reach over the lip of the front desk. A moment later, the alarm went silent. She turned back to the crowd. "Everyone, back to your rooms. Now!"

As one, the crowd dashed to the hall, creating even more havoc as they all tried to fit through the narrow passage at the same time. A lot of shouting and shoving ensued, especially when Jack Sprat's wife got stuck.

"Welcome to managing the Magdalene," Carl said, regarding Sylvia coolly. "Maybe we don't take *as* long of an extended vacation?"

She winced at the chaos in front of them. Maybe their decision was too hasty. They had no experience. They weren't Harold and Angie.

What had felt so clear and exciting a moment ago suddenly felt rash and reckless. She opened her mouth to agree but caught sight of Merri watching her. And even though they were just hand drawn black circles, Merri's eyes held such wisdom and understanding, Sylvia remembered again their earlier conversation.

Who was doing the second guessing? She smiled to herself. "Who needs the extended vacation is our judger," she said to her husband, earning a triumphant grin from her cartoon friend.

Juliet rushed up to them. "Hey, chat later. Time to get ready."

"What do we do?" Carl asked her.

"How am I supposed to know? You're the managers."

"For all of five minutes," he argued.

"Seven," she corrected.

"Don't panic," Merri said to them all. "Angie and Harold must have left instructions."

"Of course!" Sylvia headed across the room to the front desk. "I'll look for them while you three try and straighten up this mess."

In their haste to exit, several of the occupants had forgotten to retrieve pieces of their clothing and other valuables. Excalibur, a couple crowns, several scarves, and an untouched platter of granola bars were left behind, as well as Cheetah, Tarzan's chimp, still swinging from the chandelier.

Mrs. Claus moved to the center to try and coax him down as Carl and Juliet ran around, stashing items under couches and behind potted plants.

A minute later, the front door crashed open, revealing a pretty blonde backing into the lobby with an armful of luggage.

"I don't care. Leave if you want. But I'm going to make the most of this weekend, with or without you," she shouted at someone still outside.

Sylvia, Carl, Juliet, Mrs. Claus, and the chimp all froze.

"On second thought, just leave. I'll get my own ride back to town. I've had it, Logan. I'm done." Face and neck flushed with anger, she whirled around, but then caught sight of the lobby.

"Hi there," Sylvia called out cheerily from the front desk. "Welcome to the—"

But before she could finish her greeting, the young woman let out a strangled cry.

Sylvia followed the woman's stunned gaze.

Stock-still at the far end of the lobby, Mrs. Claus stood hand in hand with Cheetah. Raising their clasped hands in greeting, they both managed a nervous smile.

"So much for first impressions," Sylvia muttered.

The blonde's eyes grew wide, and her once-flushed face went white. With a choked squeak, she stumbled backwards through the front door, purse and luggage flying. The suitcase slammed against a potted plant, cracking its trunk. The purse spun through the air, landing at Mrs. Claus's feet.

She stepped over it, wincing. "Perhaps Cheetah and I had better get back to our rooms."

She and the chimp beat a quick exit.

"I think Nurse has smelling salts. I'll go get them," Juliet said, hurrying after the two.

Sylvia sighed. "Welcome to the Inn that's guaranteed to change you… one way or another."

The hinged front doors swung back, stopped by the blonde's pair of Freebirds. She was now sprawled across the pink cement of the entrance, moaning softly.

Carl cleared his throat. "I guess we better."

"Yep. We better…" Sylvia crossed the room to join him, unaware of passing a nearby alcove where a couple of new cupid statuettes sat arm-in-arm, one in a coral Hawaiian t-shirt.

Together, they opened the door.

And stepped out into the light.

ACKNOWLEDGMENTS

I am so very grateful to the angels—both seen and unseen—who have supported me and the writing of this book.

First, I want to thank my mom who has been my champion and cheerleader, inspired my love of reading and imagining, and encouraged me to go for my dreams.

I'm also very grateful to my dad who has been my greatest model for creativity and achievement.

Big hugs go to my sisters, Taira and Gina, who made themselves available for frequent "it'll only take a few minutes" meetings that more often than not turned into marathon sessions for enhancing *Keys'* content, covers, and copy. You both are the true definition of soul sister.

Speaking of big favors…thank you, Kevin Reagan, for lending me your award-winning eye and design magic to the book's gorgeous cover.

And for his skill in bringing to life the story between the covers, my gratitude to Brian Dooley, my book coach and co-adventurer into the magic of the Magdalene. This story wouldn't be what it is today without your talent, depth, and insight.

My heartfelt thanks to Morgan Gist MacDonald who believed in this book and the vision of Self-Help Story, and who supported me and this project with her skill, generosity, and savvy. Morgan, it is a gift to work with you and all the members of the Paper Raven Books team. You all are truly an oasis of excellence.

Many thanks to Denise, Breana, Ted, Mick, Dayna, and Cindy Lou who were my muses in a multitude of ways, from fairy dust to fashion, legal to literary consultation.

For their mastery and mentoring in spiritual psychology, my thanks to Drs. Ron & Mary Hulnick of the University of Santa Monica. For the spiritual insights and support, thank you John-Roger, Michael Hayes, Alisha Das Hayes, John Morton, Martin Nicario, Raymond Segrist, and the other members of my spiritual community.

My gratitude goes as well to all the individuals and couples I've had the privilege of working with—you have taught me so much about the commitment to grow and the courage to heal.

To the divine community of beings who inspire me every step of the way—your love and presence illuminate the journey Home.

And lastly, my heart goes to my husband, David. Thank you for being my playmate and partner in this extraordinary and magical life of love.

Discover the Secrets of the Magdalene Inn

AN EXCLUSIVE INVITATION & GIFT...

What Are Your Keys to Lasting Love?

Hey there!

Licia here. As the author of *Keys to the Last Resort*, I want to thank you for joining me and the rest of the crew at the Magdalene Inn.

I hope this adventure has been inspiring for you, and I'm delighted to extend a personal invitation to continue the journey together!

In my upcoming free Master Class, I'll reveal the principles and practices embedded in the novel that you can use to transform your own love story.

Whether you're a hopeless romantic like Juliet, a passionate lover like Romeo, or seeking the keys to lasting love like me, this free Master Class will open your eyes and heart to new ways of unlocking the magic in your own relationship.

Follow the link below to gain access — I can't wait to see what magic you create next!

https://www.selfhelpstory.com/masterclass

ABOUT THE AUTHOR

LICIA RESTER is the co-author of *The Soul Purpose Method* and *Virtual Event Mastery Method.* As a transformation coach and licensed marriage and family therapist, she has been privileged to support thousands of individuals in their personal and professional success. This book is the first in her Self-Help Story series, which integrates the power of storytelling with proven principles for transformation.

You can learn more about Self-Help Story at:

www.selfhelpstory.com/learnmore